# Finding Love in San Antonio

# Finding Love in San Antonio

Part of the *Finding Love In* series of books

By

# Miralee Fennell and Kimberly Rose Johnson

Finding Love in San Antonio
Published by Mountain Brook Ink
White Salmon, WA U.S.A.

The website addresses shown in this book are not intended in any way to be or imply an endorsement on the part of Mountain Brook Ink, nor do we vouch for their content.

This story is a work of fiction. All characters and events are the product of the authors' imagination. Any resemblance to any person, living or dead, is coincidental.

Scripture quotations are taken from the King James Version of the Bible. Public domain.

ISBN 978-1-953957-13-9
© 2022 Miralee Ferrell and Kimberly R Johnson

The Team: Miralee Ferrell, Alyssa Roat, Kristen Johnson, and Cindy Jackson
Cover Design: Indie Cover Design, Lynnette Bonner Designer and American Cinema International

*Mountain Brook Ink is an inspirational publisher offering fiction you can believe in.*
Printed in the United States of America

# Acknowledgments

**From Miralee**

First, I'd like to thank Chevonne O'Shaughnessy, my amazing producer who has become a friend over the last eight years of working together—it's hard to believe it's been that long! This makes book four that's become a movie, with another one on the way in my Amish series. None of this would have been possible without her and her amazing husband George, the best producer team in Hollywood!

Second, I'm so thankful for Kimberly Rose Johnson, my friend and co-writer for this book. I wasn't sure I was going to be able to pull this one off, as my life was incredibly crowded when I got the offer from Chevonne to write this. I reached out to Kimberly, who was the first author I ever signed with Mountain Brook Ink, and asked if she'd like to work on a book-to-movie project, and she said yes. We discovered it's been fun writing a book together and much easier than I had envisioned. She wrote all the scenes where we're in Sandra's point of view, and I wrote the rest. I honestly couldn't have made the book happen without her.

Third, to my ever-patient husband, Allen, who always has my back and rejoices with me when I make my word count for the day and commiserates when I don't. Thank you for being my rock in this crazy writing business that I call fun.

And finally, but most importantly, huge thanks go to the Lord for His ever-present help, wisdom, creativity, and strength to get through each day. I am blessed beyond measure to be Your child.

Thank you to all the wonderful readers who make the time to read my books. I hope you'll enjoy this new adventure Kimberly and I launched together!

**From Kimberly**

Special thanks to Miralee for inviting me to co-write this project with her. I think for perhaps the first time in my writing career, I didn't hesitate. I knew this was something I wanted to do, and I'm so glad I did. Miralee, it was great working with you on this. I thoroughly enjoyed writing Sandra's story.

Thank you, Chevonne, for continuing to produce family friendly movies!

To my husband whose support enables me to do what I love, thank you.

I can't write without the help of the Lord. Thank You, Heavenly Father, for giving me this opportunity.

# Chapter One

ADELA PACED THE FLOOR OF HER TV kitchen a few minutes prior to filming...why did her daughter's soccer game have to be so close in time to her final episode of her award-winning cooking show, *Adela Romero's Alta Cocina*? Or maybe if she was fair, she'd wonder why the filming always seemed to overlap Fabiola's games. Fabi had been patient, if not disappointed, the first one or two times Adela had arrived late in the stands, but the last couple of times, she had missed the game entirely. That could not happen again tonight.

Her director, and a man she'd grown to appreciate like a father, stepped up next to the camera and nodded her way. "Almost time, Adela. Put on that million-dollar smile now for your fans and wow them one more time."

Adela tried to push Fabi out of her mind. Mr. O'Shaughnessy was right. It was time to wow her fans, and she couldn't do that if she was worrying about her daughter. If she got out of here the second they wrapped, she'd be able to make it across Los Angeles and to the game before the halfway point of the match. Surely, Fabi would understand, especially since she didn't have any more shows to film for a few months.

"Three, two, one..." Mr. O whirled his finger in the

air, the camera came to life, and Adela mustered her brightest smile, determined to live up to her reputation.

"Today, we're making a scrumptious lamb *tamale*. It sounds harder than it is, I promise. Once your lamb has hung out in the perforated holder for ten hours, you want to remove the meat from the bone. Keep that broth, though! We're gonna use it, I swear on my daughter's reputation as a soccer player, *mi amigos*." Now where had that come from? She gave a nervous chuckle and tried to corral her runaway thoughts.

A laugh from a cameraman was quickly stifled, and Adela glanced his way. Was he laughing at her or with her? It didn't matter. She must keep her mind on her job. "In a stock pot, combine the lamb, the roasted trumpet mushrooms, *guajillo* puree, and yes, just like I promised, that beautiful, beautiful broth!" She kissed her fingers and waved her hand in the air. "Bring that to a simmer and then season with sea salt and *chile de arbol*. Let the mixture cool so it solidifies a bit. Then pour it into these tamales that have waited ever so patiently."

She scooped her filling into uncooked tamales and then started wrapping them up. "We wrap up our little *Navidad* presents one by one and put them in the oven for about forty-five minutes. And they come out like this..." She reached beneath the counter and pulled out a bunch of ready-made tamales. Then she picked up a bottle of oregano and garnished them. "I recommend a little grated Oaxaca cheese and some fresh Mexican oregano. *Delicioso!*" She sprinkled the cheese on top of the warm tamales and then picked up the tamale and took a big bite.

A little juice seeped out the side of her mouth, and she smiled. "And that is how you get my lamb tamale...all over your face." She winked at the camera and grins broke out all over the set. Adela waved at the camera. "Thanks for tuning in to another episode of *Adela Romero's Alta Cocina*. Until next time—*adios!*"

Mr. O waved his hand in the air. "And...cut!" He stepped over and gave Adela a side-hug. "Nice job! I'm sure it's going to be another winner."

"Thank you, sir. I'm glad you felt it went well." She glanced at the clock on the wall, and her pulse increased. Would she make it to the game in time? She might even make the opening of the game if traffic wasn't too bad, although that was probably wishful thinking this time of day.

The director grinned at the crew. "That's a wrap for the season, people. Good work!"

Whoops and clapping broke out from the crew, and Adela took a little bow. It was nice to be appreciated. If only she had the time to stay and chat with the crew. They had all been amazing to work with the past few months.

Mr. O stepped a little closer, dropped his voice, and then gestured to the panful of tamales. "Do you mind if we...?"

She grinned, always more than pleased when people enjoyed her cooking. It was one of the best things about this job. Sure, she liked the feedback from fans and the recognition on the streets, even the TV spots she did for publicity, but her true love was here in the kitchen— cooking for the sheer joy of it. Unfortunately, she had little time to do that these days with the demands of her job and the promotional obligations. "Sure. Help yourselves. I need to get going, though. My daughter has a game, so I won't be able to stay and join you."

Mr. O's expression fell, but he patted her arm and smiled. "Sorry to hear that. You're right. Family should come first when possible. Go enjoy your time with Fabi and give her my best. I hope they win."

Adela shot him a quick smile. "Thank you, Mr. O. I know she'll love hearing that." She could hug the man, but she wouldn't step over the professional boundaries, especially with the rest of the crew crowding around the large tray of tamales. Time to get out of here before anyone tried to draw her into the crowd. "'Bye, everyone, off to my daughter's game. Enjoy!"

Several people smiled and waved, and one who didn't have her mouth full replied as Adela headed to the door. "You'll be at our cast party, though, right?"

"Wouldn't miss it!" Adela waved over her shoulder and kept moving, straight out of the studio on the way to her car, as fast as her legs would move.

She cleared the outer doorway of the studio and almost ran into someone hurrying toward her at a fast pace. "Matias!" She studied her manager through narrowed eyes. "What brings you here? I assumed you'd be coming to the cast party, but I didn't expect to see you today."

Matias straightened his tie—an expensive one that appeared to be new. She'd never seen him anything but impeccably dressed, even the one time he'd shown up at her daughter's soccer game. "Looking for you and it's a good thing I caught you before you got to your car. I assume you were headed to your car?"

Adela gave her head a hard shake and wisps of her blond hair brushed her cheeks. "Not now, Matias. I'm barely going to make it to any of Fabiola's soccer game as it is. You know what traffic can be like this time of the afternoon. Whatever you need, it will have to wait. Now excuse me." She hated being brusque with him, but she was certain she'd told him about Fabi's game. He was a great guy and typically understanding, but when it came to business, he was—well, tenacious, unfortunately.

He touched her arm as she started to brush past him. "Wait, Adela. You didn't forget your interview today, did you?"

Her heart lurched. She remembered it now.

"With the food critic?" He winced. "I mean, food writer. Hopefully, he'll only have good things to say in his article with you, but not if you miss the interview." He arched a brow and tipped his head to the side. One perfectly groomed hair slipped out of place, and Adela bit back a smile.

"Right. The food writer. Sure. I remember. But I can do it on the phone in my car, can't I? While I'm driving to the game? I can't be late, Matias. This game is super important to Fabi." She planted her arms over her chest. She'd love to stomp her foot for emphasis, but that was something Fabi would do, not her mother.

"I'm sorry. You can't take it in the car. We set up a video call so they can use it for social media. I know it's inconvenient, but you have to take this."

She firmed her stance, not about to give in if she didn't have to. "Then reschedule. That shouldn't be too big of a deal, right?"

"I could try, but it's your hometown paper, Adela."

She blew out a breath and relaxed her stance. "Aren't you supposed to be in my corner? Make my life a little easier instead of harder?"

"I hate to do this to you, but it's going to look bad if you blow them off at the last minute without any warning. Maybe if I'd known this morning?"

Defeat hit her hard in the stomach, and she tried not to sigh yet again. She was sure she'd told him about the soccer game today. One more black mark on her mother card as far as Fabi was concerned. "Fine. Whatever. But it had better be a quick interview. I'm serious, Matias. I can't miss another game."

He held up his hands in a placating gesture. "I know. I know. We'll do the best we can."

FABIOLA ROMERO JOGGED out onto the field with the rest of her teammates to the roar of the nearly packed bleachers. She bit her lip as she slowed her pace, scanning the crowd in the area where her grandmother—and her mother whenever she happened to show up—usually sat. Her gaze landed on *Abuela* Romero and then slid a fraction to the empty seat beside her. Why was she disappointed—or surprised? After all, Mom rarely put out the effort to make her games. Her stupid job always came ahead of family. Ahead of her.

"Fabi!" Her grandmother's clear, sweet voice sang out as soon as the noise abated. She sat prim and proper, every bit the lady she was, wearing a bright, proud smile.

Fabi gestured toward her coach and then hurried toward the stands. "Abuela! It's great to see you. I wasn't sure if you'd make it." Good thing she was only sitting in the third row from the bottom, so Fabi could carry on a conversation with her.

She leaned forward. "Of course, I made it. I would never miss my granddaughter's championship game! Besides, I'll use any excuse I can get to see *mi nieta*."

Fabi grinned, feeling truly happy for the first time since she came out on the field. Then her gaze again drifted to the empty seat next to Abuela. "Where's Mom? Have you heard from her?"

Her grandmother gave her what was supposed to be a warm smile, but it was missing something. Fabi's hope plummeted. Mom wasn't coming. Exactly like she'd expected. How could Mom miss her championship game? Of all the ones this year for her mother to miss, did it have to be the most important match?

Abuela's smile grew even more forced. "She'll be here as soon as she can. She texted me. I'm guessing she hit bad traffic. You know how it can be in L.A. at rush hour."

"Yeah. Right."

"Fabiola!" Her coach's voice boomed over the crowd. "Move it." He gestured to the gathering group of her teammates.

"Talk to you later, Abuela. I'd better go." She waved

and jogged toward her coach, but all the joy of the game had faded as soon as she saw that empty seat. She doubted Mom would make it before half-time ended, if then. After the fourth missed game, she'd learned not to count on Mom when it came to attending things that were important to her. Fabi lifted her chin and squared her shoulders. She wasn't going to let it get to her. Not this time, and not ever again.

# Chapter Two

ADELA PUT THE FINISHING TOUCHES ON her makeup...not that she really needed to do it over again, but the bright lights of the kitchen studio had put a bit of shine on her face that wouldn't put her at her best on a video interview. She picked up her phone and looked at the clock for what must be the tenth time since Matias had snagged her leaving the studio. The game had started fifteen minutes ago, and she'd still have to deal with rush hour traffic once she finished this interview. This had better be the best interview she'd ever had.

Her laptop pinged, and a face filled the screen. Adela was momentarily startled. She'd seen pictures of David Agraponte, of course, but she'd never spoken to the man that she could remember. Handsome. Maybe mid-thirties and definitely of Mexican-American descent, like her. Wow. She shook off the reaction and pasted on her best professional smile. "Good afternoon!"

"Greetings, Ms. Romero. It's nice to see you. I'm a fan of your shows. I'm David Agraponte." He tipped his dark head in a gesture of greeting and then gave her a brilliant smile that left her blinking rapidly to clear her thoughts so she could reply.

"Uh. Thanks. But it's Adela, not Ms. Romero. It's

nice to meet you as well. May I call you David or would you prefer Mr. Agraponte?" She tried to match his smile, but her gaze had drifted to her phone again, with the lit-up time display, and she guessed her smile might look more like a grimace.

"Sounds good to me, Adela. I appreciate you giving me some of your valuable time today."

What was it about the slight emphasis on the word valuable that made her sit up a bit straighter and question the validity of his words? She started to narrow her eyes but remembered this was being filmed and opened them wide. "Of course. It's always nice to talk to someone from my hometown. Now, what would you like to know?" She flicked a glance at Matias who gave her a quick thumbs up and mouthed, "Good job!"

David leaned back a few inches in what appeared to be a cushy leather desk chair. "Let's talk *Alta Cocina*. I hear you just wrapped up another season. Congratulations!"

Warmth spread through Adela. It was always nice to hear positives about her show, and she guessed that's where this was heading based on the little smile he'd given her after the congratulations. "Yes, thank you. It was my favorite season so far."

He gave a slight nod. "So your cooking career started in humble kitchens around San Antonio, correct?" He touched his fingertips together and brought them up to his lips. "Or at least so my research has revealed."

She smiled. "It sounds as though you've definitely done your due diligence for this interview. That's correct."

He lowered his arms to his desk and leaned forward, his brows arched and a slight frown tugging at his lips. "Yet, the dishes you choose do little to honor the rich traditions of our local heritage. Instead, they seem to cater to the rich. There are few of your recipes that are affordable for the average person to make, isn't that true?"

DAVID WAITED, WONDERING if this Adela would dodge the question or answer honestly. Probably give a dodge with excuses to follow. She did her best by trying to please everyone and more of that kind of drivel. These actresses were all alike. Entitled. Elitist. Thinking the world owed them—but he knew her roots went back to the common person with a hardworking family. How had she changed so much? Why wasn't she cooking the way he knew she'd been taught? He wouldn't pull any punches in this interview. He'd say it the way he saw it. She wasn't trying to cater to the average viewer, but to the rich.

"Yes." She shook her head and drew back from the screen. "Wait. What? Why in the world would you say that?" Her gorgeous eyes widened, and she appeared to stare straight into David's soul.

He squirmed a bit, but no way was he going to back down. "Here's an example. You've become increasingly out of touch with your mainstream audience. On recent episodes you made Bluefin Tuna *Ceviche*, truffle *huevos rancheros*, Kobe beef *empanadas*..." Let's see what she'd have to say about that.

"Yes. And that's a problem, why?" She continued to stare into his eyes without so much as flinching.

He could almost feel the outrage simmering over the Internet feed. "What's wrong is that I'd have to fly overseas for some of the ingredients. Do you call those dishes that the common person can afford to make?"

Her eyes narrowed only slightly, but he didn't miss the tightening of her facial muscles. "All right, I'll give you the point that not everyone can pick up Japanese beef at their local supermarket."

He knew he was striking a nerve, but he had to see this interview through. It was important to get at the truth, even though he might feel a slight twinge of guilt and sympathy for broadsiding her and not taking this interview where she obviously had expected it to go. "In your first series, here in San Antonio, *Adela's Kitchen*, you featured simple, delicious recipes. Have you forgotten where you came from and who your audience is?"

Adela took two deep breaths. Was she trying to control herself or trying to figure out what to say to his question? She tipped her head to one side. "Of course not. But sometimes the network has certain recipes they want me to try."

He felt a bit of triumph at uncovering the truth, but it was mixed with a hint of sadness. "So you admit the recipes aren't your own?"

This time she did narrow her eyes. "You didn't allow me to finish. May I please continue?"

He tried not to smile. "Certainly." He drew in a deep breath and took a second to think. "And I apologize. I didn't mean to upset you, but I was hoping to bring you back to your roots."

Matias, Adela's manager suddenly loomed over Adela's shoulder wearing an ingratiating smile. "David, let's move on from this question. How about you ask Adela about some of her favorite recipes or possibly the places she's enjoyed the most on her food tours."

Adela pressed her lips together for a second before she responded. "Thank you, Matias, but I can handle this, and I'd like to answer whatever questions he cares to ask. Mr. Agraponte, I can assure you I stand behind every recipe I demonstrate on my show. Some of them might be fancier than others, and they might not all be for the general population, but those would be considered appropriate for entertaining. I see nothing wrong with sharing more exquisite dishes along with ones that would appeal to the average person."

He quirked a brow. "So you admit you're more of an entertainer than a chef...that's what you're saying, yes?"

"No. It most certainly is not what I'm saying." She gave a bright, if not completely authentic, smile. "I am first and foremost a chef. I love cooking. It's always been my passion. Nothing comes ahead of that."

"I see. Then can you tell me, Adela, why you choose to use some of your network's recipes instead of your own?" He leaned back and crossed his arms, hoping she'd give him an honest answer this time and not one even the least discerning viewer could see through.

She sat as though turned to stone, her lips parting but no words coming out.

Matias stepped in again and his low voice came through. "I'm so sorry, Mr. Agraponte, but Adela has another appointment and must leave now. Thank you for the interview."

David couldn't say he was surprised, but he had to try one more time. "Thank you, Adela. May I ask one more question before you go?"

The connection broke and the screen went blank. She'd closed her device, the equivalent of hanging up on him. Well, he couldn't say he didn't have it coming after those pointed questions that put her on the spot. If only he didn't have a boss to please—maybe that interview would have gone a little differently. Oh well, all part of the job. But the look on her face when he'd asked her that last question made him just a little bit sick to his stomach.

ADELA SAT AT her dressing table and steamed for a full minute. The nerve of that man. He was making her miss her daughter's game *and* criticizing her? What kind of interview was this, anyway?

Matias pulled in a deep breath and then exhaled. "Well, that was ..."

"Yeah, I know." Adela swung around on her chair and faced him. "My worst interview ever."

"No..." Matias scratched his chin but avoided her eyes.

"Who does he think he is, talking to me like that? Why would he even ask for an interview? Was his goal to sabotage my show or what?"

Matias held up his hands, palms out. "Hey, don't listen to him. You're killing it out there with your fans.

14

They're not going to care what some reporter says in a video interview. Forget it. It's not worth worrying about."

"Yeah. Whatever." She grabbed her phone, glanced at it, and gasped. "Fabi's game! By the time I get through traffic...I need to go, Matias. Now." She dashed for the door, ignoring his protest that he wanted to talk about damage control. Damage control? Hadn't he just said her fans wouldn't care? Whatever. Right now, she didn't care at all. Fabi was the only thing that mattered, and she'd already blown that, big time.

# Chapter Three

PERSPIRATION DRIPPED DOWN FABI'S HAIRLINE AS she stood poised on the soccer field. A shrill whistle split the air as her coach called for a brief timeout to send in another player. Fabi took a second to glance at the stands, seeking out the seat next to her abuela. Surely, her mother had arrived by now. Empty.

Her shoulders slumped. What did she expect? Why did she get her hopes up for this last match? Stupid, that's what. Fabi turned away to stare at the scoreboard. The fourth quarter with forty seconds to play. They were tied 2-2. The tension in the air reached from the players clear to the stands as everyone either sat or stood, poised for the final seconds of the game. She had to forget about her mother. She couldn't blow the last of the game for her teammates.

The whistle sounded again, shrill and piercing. She shook her head, trying to clear it of disappointment. Time to get her attention back on the game. Two of the opposing team kicked the ball back and forth, keeping control as they worked their way toward Fabi's team's goal. Her adrenaline surged, and Fabi raced toward the ball. She had to intercept the players before they could kick it in and win the game.

She darted toward the closest striker, feinting toward one then over to the next before they realized what she was doing. In a matter of seconds, she charged the player, lightly bumping her with her shoulder. Then she tapped the ball to the side. It only took her a second, and she had control. Fabi dribbled down the edge of the field on her own, but she knew at least a couple of her teammates would be fanning out to protect her. She could faintly hear the crowd roaring as she ran, but her entire concentration stayed on the ball—and her attention forward on the goal of the opposing team.

Only three more strides! One of the strikers moved in to steal the ball, but Fabi swiveled and kept control. One more stride and she kicked. It went straight and true—over to her striker teammate who was waiting in front of the goal. Her teammate shot the ball right between the goalie's legs and into the net behind. They scored!

The crowd went wild as the buzzer sounded, ending the game. Their team had done it! They'd won the finals. Her heart surged with joy as her teammates surrounded the striker, pounding her on the back and shouting congratulations. Fabi stayed on the fringes, not caring that they weren't giving her as much credit for the steal. Mom hadn't shown up in time to see her help the team win, and that hurt. She raised her chin. No. She wouldn't allow herself to be hurt again. Enough. She ran toward her team as they started breaking apart. It was time to congratulate the other team. She trotted along the line, slapping hands as she moved but kept glancing at the stands. Abuela stood, waving her arms, a huge grin plastered on her face.

Fabi raised a hand and waved, but her heart wasn't in it.

As soon as she reached the end of the line of players, she hurried toward the stands. At least she could give her grandmother a hug.

Abuela met her on the grass and threw her arms around her. "You did great, *mi amor*! You won the game!"

Fabi pulled back and tried not to grin. Abuela didn't know much about soccer, but she loved watching Fabi play. "I had an assist. I didn't score the goal."

"But you took the ball away from the other team, so you did win the game. They would have scored the goal had you not done so." She touched Fabi's cheek. "Pretty, smart, and humble, all in one. You are a star. I'm so proud of you."

ADELA COULD SEE the players leaving the field and the crowd starting to disperse as soon as she hit the edge of the parking lot. No! She'd missed the game. She'd so hoped she'd at least make it to the final quarter so she could watch her baby play. Her gaze searched the crowd as she ran onto the edge of the field. Had Fabi already left for the locker room to change? She glanced at the score board. The home team had won! If only she'd been here to see it. It was David's fault...and Matias. Why had her manager scheduled an interview when he knew Fabi had a game?

She skidded to a halt as her gaze landed on her mother-in-law and Fabi just breaking apart from a hug. Rushing over, she reached out to draw her girl into her arms.

18

Fabi took a step back. "Mom."

Adela stepped toward her and threw her arms around her, but her daughter stood stiff and unresponsive. Adela bit her lip and moved away. "I'm so sorry. I meant to be here, truly I did. The traffic was bad. Worse than usual at this time of day." She took a deep breath and gave what she hoped was an excited smile. "Yay! You won! I knew your team could do it with you helping. You've worked so hard this season. You deserved this."

Fabi's expression remained flat, unreadable. "How would you know? You're never at my practices or most of my games."

Abuela Soccoro Romero stepped closer and slipped her hand around Fabi's arm. "Fabi."

Adela's eyes widened. "I tried, baby. I really did. But I had to work. After the final shoot for my show, Matias scheduled an interview with a local paper."

"Yeah. Right." Fabi smirked. "There's always work. And it always comes first, doesn't it? You said you'd be here this time. You promised."

Adela didn't know whether to cry or say something about her daughter's snippy tone. Maybe another tactic would work better. She reached out and touched Fabi's hair. "Let's go celebrate. You can pick the place. You, me, Abuela, and any of your friends you'd like to invite. Come on. You earned this."

Fabi shook her head. "I just want to go home. I'll grab my stuff and ride with Abuela. You don't need to hang around." She walked off and joined her teammates leaving the field.

Adela's shoulders slumped. "I blew it this time, didn't I?"

She didn't expect anyone to answer, but a soft hand touched hers and then grasped it. "Yes, mi amor. You did. But I'm glad this time you are willing to admit it."

ADELA HELD UP her hand when Soccoro started to rise from the kitchen table where they'd finished their meal. "No, I'm clearing up tonight. This is my treat for you both. Fabi had a fantastic game." She tossed a warm smile at her daughter, praying she'd get one in return, but Fabi's face remained the same it had been since the game. Tight and flat, as though she were reining in her emotions and refusing to allow them to escape. Adela understood. She hadn't been there for her daughter the way she knew she should be. Girls needed their moms, and her job had been all absorbing. But things would be different now that this season had ended.

Their upcoming summer in San Antonio would be welcome to Fabi, even if it did bring back too many painful memories to Adela's own heart. She glanced at a glassed-in cupboard above the granite countertop that housed some of her most treasured crystal and a picture of her with Mauricio and Fabi when her daughter was only nine. She bit her lip. Time to let go of the past and move on. Her sweet husband had been gone for three years now. She couldn't keep grieving.

Fabi pushed her chair back from the table. "I think I'll go to my room now." She swiveled her head and barely glanced at Adela. "May I be excused?"

"Um...I bought homemade ice cream from that place we love so much in Silverton. I even got your favorite flavor—strawberry with big chunks of real strawberries in it. Why don't you wait a few more minutes and have a bowl?" Her voice sounded too hopeful—almost whiney, but Adela couldn't help it. Her heart hurt at the thought of her baby going to her room and being alone after her big win this afternoon. This should have been a happy celebration with friends, cake and ice cream, and lots of laughter.

"No, thanks. I'm tired. It's been a busy week with practices and keeping up with my homework. 'Night, Abuela. Thank you for coming to my match today." She cast Adela a quick look and then headed for the door leading to her bedroom.

Adela sat for a moment feeling as though her limbs were paralyzed. She drew in a long, shaky breath and then tried to smile. "Let me get that ice cream for you, Soccoro. Looks like we have more than enough for the two of us."

Her mother-in-law reached across the table and placed her warm hand over Adela's. "Let me. You've done enough with preparing this wonderful meal and buying the ice cream."

Adela slumped back into her chair. "Thank you. I'm blowing this whole single-parenting thing, aren't I? You'd think after three years that I'd have the hang of it by now." She shook her head. "From the look on Fabi's face when she left, I'm not even close."

Soccoro set down a bowl of ice cream in front of

Adela and then took her place and scooped up a big spoonful. "No, you're not blowing it. I know you're doing the best you can with the expectations you have at work. It's hard to be a working parent."

"Tell that to Fabi." Adela regretted the words as soon as they left her lips. "Sorry. That wasn't fair." She took a bite of the ice cream, but somehow it wasn't quite as good as she'd remembered.

Soccoro patted Adela's shoulder, her gaze warm and kind. "Remember, Mauricio loved you and so do Fabi and I. You shouldn't be so hard on yourself, *mija*. Many single parents struggle with trying to balance their work and home life, especially when they have children, not to mention such a demanding career as yours."

"I'm not sure Fabi sees it that way, but thank you for your love and support." Adela lifted another scoop to her mouth. Somehow, the taste had improved since the last bite.

"Hmm—this really is the best ice cream in the city." Soccoro dabbed at her lips with a napkin and beamed, her face almost glowing. "I can't wait to have the two of you back in San Antonio with me for the summer. It's been too long."

Adela allowed a tentative smile to respond to Soccoro's enthusiasm. "Fabi seems pretty excited about it too. It's all she's talked about—when she's talked, that is."

"And you? How do you feel about returning?"

Adela hesitated and then blurted, "I guess I have mixed feelings. There's so much I love about that city— the river walk, the Alamo and all the history there—but facing it without Mauricio is kind of scary. Well, maybe not scary, but sad, you know?"

"I do. But as hard as it is, trying to avoid your memories won't help. Going back and facing them head-on will help you heal. Let yourself remember all the good times, and even the ones that weren't perfect. Every marriage has them, right? It's time for you to move on mija. I loved him too, but I know he wouldn't want you to continue to grieve and put your life on hold for so long."

"I agree. Like always, Soccoro, you speak wisdom." She sat up a bit straighter and allowed a big smile to curve her lips. "I'm also excited to see the renovations at Romero's. The pictures of the new look at your restaurant look great!"

Soccoro nodded. "It was all my niece Sandra's idea. She's managing things for me while I'm away, and she felt the changes would bring in more business."

Adela arched a brow. Of course, she remembered Sandra, Mauricio's cousin, so a member of the family — her cousin-in-law to be exact. A capable young woman with a passion for Soccoro's business, but she didn't remember the restaurant thriving the last time she was there. Hopefully, that had changed. "Has it made a difference having her in charge and making the changes she's requested?"

Soccoro bit her lip and slowly shook her head. "No. Not yet."

# Chapter Four

"YOU ARE SMART, AND YOU CAN do anything you put your mind to." Sandra Soto added a barrette to her long hair and then ran her hand down the sides of her white sundress as she stared at her reflection in the vintage entryway mirror of her abuela's house. Maybe if Sandra gave herself the pep-talk enough times, she'd figure out what kept Romero's, the Mexican diner where she was the assistant manager, from turning a profit. One of her college professors had insisted positive self-talk was the key to success. So far it wasn't working, but she wouldn't give up. It had to work sooner or later. At least she hoped so.

"Is that you, Sandra?" Abuela asked.

Sandra sighed. "*Sí*. Yes. I'm on my way out." She loved her abuela, but there were days she wished she lived alone rather than under her grandmother's watchful eye. It wouldn't be so bad except she had fixated on Sandra's love life, or lack thereof.

"Come here so I can see you when I'm talking to you. I have some exciting news."

Sandra was going to be late, but she wouldn't disrespect her grandmother. She plopped her boho style purse onto the mid-century modern console table beneath the mirror and strode across the terra cotta tile flooring into the family room. Sunlight streamed in from the sliding glass door, spotlighting the dust in the air.

She had a suspicion Abuela's exciting news had to do with the latest man she'd set up with a date for Sandra. Her grandmother was a handful at the best of times, but lately, she had become unbearable with her constant meddling. If Sandra wanted a man in her life, she'd use a dating app like everyone else. She didn't need to be set up.

Sandra stopped in front of her grandmother's worn, green recliner where she often sat to enjoy her morning coffee while watching birds in the lush backyard.

"Why are you leaving so early?" Abuela raised her brows.

"I'm meeting Mya for coffee, and then I need to stop for groceries on my way to the diner." Thankfully, the coffee shop was in the right direction to make a stop at the grocery store easy. "Manny threw a stink last night about needing fresher vegetables." She resisted rolling her eyes. The cook at Romero's was temperamental and a thorn in her side. He was good, but they could do better if they only had the money to pay for a topnotch chef. If that was possible, then the diner would be a huge success like it was when her *tío* was alive.

Sandra had suggested everything she could think of to improve business. She'd thought for sure remodeling the dining area of the Mexican diner would do the trick, but it had only helped for a short while. So far, her classes in restaurant management had not helped. What would it take to get Romero's back to its glory days? *Tía* Soccoro didn't have the same passion her husband had had for the business.

Abuela placed her empty coffee cup on the end table that matched the console table in the entryway. "You're wasting time at that diner. Soccoro should have closed it when Adela moved to Hollywood to be a famous TV chef."

She cringed at the mention of Adela. Okay, she might be a little jealous of the woman's success, but at least David had put Adela in her place. She sighed and pushed the thought away. Hating on Adela was a waste of time and put her in a rotten mood.

Abuela waved a finger at Sandra and handed Sandra a business card. "What you need is a husband."

"Who's this?" She read the card for some attorney named Anthony. "Are you in legal trouble?" Her stomach lurched. How would she deal with Abuela's legal issue and the diner?

"No, *Niña*. He's a friend's grandson. He's *muy guapo*. Call him. He's expecting you."

Relief, quickly replaced with frustration, shot through her. "Abuela! I don't care how handsome he is. I'm not looking for a man. You have to stop setting me up with your friends' grandsons. The diner takes all my time."

Abuela crossed her arms. "You should be more concerned about starting a family. Your mother, God rest her soul, would expect nothing less."

Sandra squeezed her eyes closed. Abuela knew how

to get her to do what she wanted even if it was a low blow. Her heart hurt at the mention of her mom. She took a cleansing breath and then opened her eyes. "If I call him, will you promise to stop trying to set me up?"

Abuela set her jaw and shrugged. "You'll like this one."

Sandra giggled. It was no laughing manner, but she either laughed or cried, and she would choose laughter any day over crying. She pulled her smart phone from the pocket of her sundress and called the number handwritten on the back of the card.

"Anthony speaking." His deep velvety voice rumbled.

Sandra froze. If he looked half as good as he sounded… She cleared her throat. "Hi. This is Sandra Soto. I believe you were expecting my call. My grandmother—"

"Right. You caught me at a bad time. I'm on my way to meet with a client."

"On a Saturday?" Didn't attorneys work weekdays? Maybe he was a criminal attorney and had to meet his client at the jail.

"I answer the call for help whenever I'm needed. Are you free to meet for coffee this afternoon?"

"No. I'll be working. My mornings are my own until ten."

"Okay. How about brunch tomorrow? Technically breakfast, but the place I have in mind does a brunch menu on Sundays."

She shrugged as if the man could see her. Romero's

was closed on Sundays, but there was no sense in telling him that. "Sure." She had a brunch date. Much better than a coffee date, assuming the guy was as great as her abuela implied. If the restaurant was a good one, she might even pick up an idea on how to improve Romero's.

"Great. I'll text the details. See you tomorrow."

She tucked the phone back into her pocket and then looked at her grandmother who wore a satisfied smile. "We're meeting for brunch tomorrow. Happy?" For the first time, she didn't dread a blind date. Breakfast was her favorite meal, and she wouldn't mind listening to that man's voice for a couple of hours.

"Yes, I'm happy. I think you'll like this one." Abuela's eyes twinkled.

Sandra placed a kiss on the top of her grandma's head. "I love you, even if you do meddle. If you have an emergency, call me." Not that she could leave work, but their neighbor who was close in age to her grandmother offered to check in on Abuela. So far, Sandra had resisted asking Peter since she had the impression that he was actually interested in her grandmother romantically. She shuddered at the idea of her abuela being romantically involved with any man. Sixty-five seemed too old for romance to her, but what did she know?

She shouldered her purse and then strolled out the door and onto the front porch. She breathed in the sweet scent of the wisteria trailing over the garage. A warm breeze rustled the leaves of the blooming crepe myrtle that bordered the courtyard facing the sidewalk. Her sundress brushed her knees. She should wear practical jeans considering where she worked, but she loved dresses.

She pulled car keys from her purse and then strode to her light blue, vintage pickup in the driveway and climbed inside. Mya was going to be furious with her. There was late and then there was late. She shot off a text that she was on her way.

Fifteen minutes later she strolled into the corner coffee shop on the fringe of downtown San Antonio. The concrete floors and desert-colored inspired walls welcomed her. She waved to Mya who sat at a small round table for two in the center of the space. "I'm going to order my drink."

Mya nodded, looking none too happy.

She smiled at Lucinda, a college acquaintance who ran the register. "How's it going?"

"Not bad. I have one final exam left. How about you?"

"I graduated last year."

"No wonder I never see you on campus. What can I get for you?"

"A large iced tea." She paid and then strolled over to Mya and sat. "Sorry I'm late. Thanks for waiting. My grandmother—"

Mya raised her hand palm out. "Enough said." Her face softened with compassion. "What did she do this time?"

Sandra chuckled. "Nothing much, just set me up with an attorney."

Mya's dark brows touched her fringed bangs. "You

don't sound upset. What's different about this one?"

Lucinda delivered her tea. "Enjoy." She turned and walked back to the counter.

"Thanks." Sandra called after Lucinda and then turned her attention to Mya's question. "I liked his voice."

Mya laughed. "You're kidding?"

"What's so funny?"

"You agreed to go out with him because he has a great voice?"

Sandra shrugged. "Wouldn't you want to talk with someone whose voice was easy to listen to? I'm serious. He should have had a career in radio. I'm intrigued. Besides, it's a brunch date. You know I could eat breakfast three times a day."

Mya giggled. "Okay. I get it. Let me know how it goes. Maybe he has a friend for me."

"I will, but you know I'm not interested in a relationship." She'd said the words so many times, she finally believed them. What would she do if there was a spark with Anthony? She took a long draw from the straw, guzzling half her drink.

"What's your hurry?" Mya asked.

"I have to stop at the grocery store for supplies before work." If she'd been only fashionably late, she'd have time to relax longer, but as it stood, she'd been well past late.

Mya nodded. "Manny still giving you grief?"

"You know it. Honestly, I'd like to fire him and hire someone without an attitude and whose cooking would draw people in from miles around." She sighed. Maybe

Abuela was right, and she was wasting her time at Romero's. No, something you loved was never a waste of time.

"Maybe you should place an ad for a chef."

"And risk Manny seeing it?" She shuddered. "No, thank you. Besides, my aunt would have a fit if I fired him."

"Does she know what he's like?" Mya wrapped a manicured hand around her coffee cup. She must have gotten one of her co-workers to do her nails.

"Of course." A part of her blamed Tía Soccoro for the debacle with Manny. A piece of her aunt died when her husband passed and she lost her passion for the diner. It was too bad too, because the restaurant had so much potential. She tapped the table. "I'm really sorry, but I have to cut short our visit today."

"It's fine. I have a client soon anyway." Mya stood.

Sandra hugged Mya. "I promise I won't be late next time."

They walked to the door.

"Ha. You're always late."

Sandra winced. "Only fashionably late." Though today, she'd been running late to begin with. The call to Anthony and talking with Grandma put her way behind. She pushed out the door. "Same time next week?"

"Yes."

"I'm serious. I promise to be on time." She'd be sure to set her alarm fifteen minutes early.

"I'll believe it when I see it." Mya waved and strode toward her little black hatchback.

Sandra would prove to Mya she could be on time.

Next week, she'd be five minutes early. Maybe she should set the alarm for thirty minutes early to be safe. She marched to her pickup, determined to get to the grocery store and to Romero's before Manny showed up. If she provided what he asked for and was there to greet him with an espresso and a smile, maybe he would actually be nice today.

"I CAN'T BELIEVE we get to spend the whole summer here!" Fabi peered through the passenger window in the backseat of Socorro's car as they cruised the streets of San Antonio.

Adela smiled at Soccoro from the front seat. It was so nice to hear her girl happy again—such a huge difference from a few days ago when she'd missed Fabi's final soccer match. "It is good, isn't it, sweet girl? I have to admit, I've missed this town more than I realized I would."

Fabi squealed and pointed. "Look! We're almost to the Alamo. Can we stop, please...pretty please?" She bounced in her seat. Bright flags waved in the breeze and old buildings loomed up ahead. "That's only a couple of blocks from the River Walk. It's been forever since we rode on one of the little boats along the walk. It would be so much fun!"

Adela lowered her window and gazed out at the historic section as Soccoro slowed the car and raised her brows. The old mission building and the remnants of the garrison that housed the soldiers never failed to stir

Adela. The Alamo and the River Walk were two of her favorite places in San Antonio as well, not to mention the restaurants and little shops that lined the walk. "Not now, Fabi. But soon, I promise." She glanced at her daughter, hoping for a bright smile.

Fabi's grin had faded, replaced with a frown.

"I promise, okay?"

"Yeah, whatever. I've heard that before." Fabi turned her head and refused to meet Adela's gaze.

Maybe a change of subject was in order. "I can't believe the humidity." Adela rolled up her window.

"Oh, please. It's a lot better than the smog in Los Angeles. It's nasty. At least the air smells better here." Soccoro wrinkled her nose. "A little humidity never killed anyone, you know."

Soccoro slowed the car and turned a corner. Adela sat up straight and pointed at a little taco stand mid-way down the block. "Soccoro, stop!"

"What is it?"

"It's Tacos Rápidos. Mauricio always came here the very first thing when we came to town."

"Yay! Tacos Rápidos! That sounds good." Fabi's gloom had suddenly disappeared, and she was back to bouncing in her seat again.

Soccoro slowed, but they'd already passed the old truck with the run-down picnic tables in a small cleared space set back from the sidewalk. Two people waited at the window, and a smiling Latino man handed an order to the first one in line.

A few minutes later, it was Adela's turn to order as

Soccoro and Fabi held a place at one of the tables. "Two *carnitas* tacos, two *tinga de polla* tacos, two Cokes, and for me three *lengua* tacos and a watermelon *agua fresca*." She slid two twenties across the beat-up wood opening.

"That's exactly what I planned to order," a man behind Adela spoke.

She spun around to stare at...*David*.

"Oh...sorry, I didn't mean to intrude."

"It's you. The food critic." She tried not to glare as her agent's voice echoed through her head urging her to always smile and keep the reviewers and critics happy, but it was hard with this man, especially after his last interview.

He arched his brows. "The name is David, actually." He held out his hand as though he wanted to shake hers.

She planted her fists on her hips. "You ambushed me in that interview, and I didn't appreciate that at all."

A small smile played at the corners of his lips. "I wouldn't say ambushed, exactly. I asked a few creative, possibly challenging questions, but isn't that what a good reporter is supposed to do?" He nodded at the taco stand. "So, what are you doing eating at this place? I wouldn't think you'd be caught dead eating anywhere like this."

She narrowed her eyes. "Then clearly you don't know me nearly as well as you seem to think you do."

"*Disculpe*, miss, here's your change. You are holding up the line." The man taking the orders held out her change and then waved behind Adela.

She peeked over David's shoulder, noticing the people staring and a few who whispered to each other.

34

"Oh. I'm so sorry." She turned back to the man and took the bag and tray of drinks he held out to her. "Thank you. I apologize for holding you up. Keep the change." She gave David a curt nod and forced a smile, which he returned with a wide grin. Then she stalked away to the table where her family waited.

Adela slid onto the hard, wooden seat and distributed the food, but she no longer felt as hungry or as excited about being here as she had when they'd stopped.

Fabi unwrapped her taco. "Who were you talking to, Mom? Someone who recognized you from your show?"

"No one important. Let's eat. This smells as good as I remember." Adela bit into her lengua taco and shut her eyes. "Hmm...heavenly." She would simply ignore people like David the food critic and go on with her own life. "This was worth coming back to San Antonio for."

Fabi giggled and took another bite of her taco, happier than Adela had seen her in a long time. Definitely worth coming to San Antonio for if it made her girl this happy.

# Chapter Five

"I TOLD YOU I CAN'T WORK like this!" Manny waved his arms while standing in the worn-out kitchen at Romero's. "Look at that grill."

"It's clean and serviceable." Sandra plastered on a smile. Those were the only nice things she could say about that blast from the past. At least the dining space had been updated with white tabletops, fresh paint, gleaming windows, vibrant decorations, and red chairs. The southwest colors on the walls all worked to brighten the space.

He swore in Spanish.

Sandra winced, raised her chin, and laced her fingers behind her back. "All the appliances work, and I bought everything on your list." She would not allow this man to intimidate her. She was the boss, at least until Tía Soccoro returned from California.

He muttered something she missed—probably for the best.

When he didn't say anything more, she fled past the counter that divided the kitchen from the dining room, unlocked the door, and flipped the sign to open. "Okay, hungry people. Come and get it." She took her position behind the counter ready to take orders. Hopefully, they'd have customers. Business had been too slow.

The door opened and a couple strode inside hand-in-hand.

She grinned. "*Buenos días.* Welcome to Romero's. I'll take your order whenever you're ready."

Ignoring her, they looked adoringly into one another's eyes.

Sandra nearly gagged. These two had it bad. She averted her gaze and hoped they'd focus on the reason they were there. She cleared her throat.

The man pulled his gaze from the woman at his side. "We'll take two of today's special and two large waters."

She collected his money and then handed him two water cups. She hated when people only wanted water. It cost them money rather than made them money, but free water was good for business.

After the lunch "rush" she wiped down the tables and took out the trash. Worry niggled at her. What was she going to tell Tía Soccoro? If things didn't turn around soon, there would no longer be a Romero's. Her stomach knotted at the thought.

Someone cleared his throat.

She turned and faced Manny. "Did you need something?"

"If you expect me to work in these conditions, I want a raise."

"You know I can't pay more."

He tossed his apron onto the prep counter. "I quit." He strode out the door without a backward glance.

Fear filled her. She wasn't a cook. What was she going to do?

# Chapter Six

ADELA GAZED OUT THE WINDOW AT all the familiar sights as they passed. Bright colors, the water from the Riverwalk in the distance, the Alamo, and at last, the place she'd both longed to see and dreaded. She wasn't sure her heart could handle walking into the building she hadn't entered since her husband's death.

"*Aquí está* Romero's!" Soccoro slipped from behind the wheel of her car and stood to face her restaurant as a proud smile lighted her face. "We are here at last."

Adela placed her arm across Fabi's shoulders and gave her daughter a hug. "Exciting, yes? To be back here again after so long."

Fabi nodded. "It feels like coming home. I'm so glad you agreed to leave L.A. and come to San Antonio for the summer. This is like a dream come true, Mom." She turned and wrapped her arms around Adela's waist and retuned the hug.

Adela's heart swelled with love and gratitude. God was good. She'd prayed and made the right decision to come back, even though some of the memories of her amazing husband would still hurt, it was time to move on—time to let go and heal. "Soccoro! You painted the building. It looks so fresh and clean. I love it!" Her gaze roamed over the bright colors on the one-story building which worked well with the partial brick siding. Even the parking area was free of debris and appeared fresh and clean. The windows sparkled as though recently washed and the entire building seemed to send out a warm welcome. How could people *not* come to this amazing place to eat?

Soccoro put her hand on Adela's shoulder. "It is good to be back—good to have the two of you here with me. Together, we will make this place successful again, sí? Let's go see what's happening inside, and you can tell me what you think of the place with the renovations Sandra suggested."

They walked through the double glass doors, and her gaze roamed the large dining room—painted brick lined one wall and bright oranges, reds, and yellows added color to the area. Adela strolled over to a wall that showcased a dozen or more framed photos—customers that had been special to Soccoro and her husband, as well as family photos with herself, Fabi, and Mauricio. A small surge of sadness assailed her, but she pushed it away. This was a new beginning...she and Fabi were back in the city Mauricio had loved so much, and she'd make the most of this summer, whatever it took. Voices behind her brought her back to the present. Soccoro and Fabi had stopped next to a young woman.

"Soccoro, you're back! I'm so glad you made it."

"Sandra, good to see you. Do you remember Fabi? Her father was your cousin. It's been a while since she's been in San Antonio." Soccoro peered at Sandra. "What's wrong with you? Your face is all pinched and looks like you swallowed a *habanero*."

Sandra, a slender brunette with long, wavy hair, gave a curt nod to Fabi. "Hi." She drew in a deep breath and slowly let it out. "Manny quit."

"What?" Soccoro's lips drew into a tight line. "Why?"

Adela stepped up beside Fabi and smiled. "Hi, Sandra. Who's Manny?"

Sandra gave her a stiff nod. "Pinche Manual, our head cook. Or he was our head cook until he quit."

"I thought you were taking care of things here. How did that happen?" Soccoro crossed her arms over her chest and let out a huff.

"I was. Things were going well until now."

"And what happened now that changed that?" Soccoro waved her hands in the air.

"He wanted a raise, and I couldn't give it to him. He was in a bad mood all morning, and when I said no, he walked out."

Adela looked from one woman to the next. "You can't give him a small raise to make him happy?"

Sandra raised a brow. "No."

Soccoro shook her head. "And he knows that we can't. He must have asked knowing you'd say no."

"What do we do now?" Sandra waved at the dining room. "People will start coming in for dinner any time, and we have no one to cook."

"I can cook for a day or two, and we can try to talk sense into Manny. I doubt he has another job to go to, so maybe we can get him back."

"It's been too long since you've cooked, Soccoro."
Sandra bit her lip. "I'm not sure..."

Soccoro shrugged. "It can't be too much different
from riding a *bicicleta*. You never forget, sí?" Her gaze
drifted to Adela. "Unless..." A twinkle sparkled in her
eyes. "Adela is willing to cook."

"Mom?" Fabi squealed and nudged Adela with her
elbow. "Cool!"

"Adela?" Sandra's mouth dropped open as she
stared.

"Me?" Adela's breath quickened, and she looked
from two hopeful faces to one shocked one.

Soccoro touched Adela's hand. "For old time's sake.
We're in a bad spot here, mija, and we could use your
help. Please?"

"Yeah, Mom, please?" Fabi was bouncing on her toes
now and grinning.

Sandra shook her head, her dark hair flying. "What
does she know about diner cooking? This isn't a set in
Hollywood, you know."

"Adela was the best cook Romero's ever had back in
the day. She's only become more skilled since then, right,
Adela?" Soccoro turned to look at Adela, her eyes
pleading.

With a sigh, Adela gave in. She wouldn't hurt
Soccoro for the world, and there didn't appear to be a lot
of choices. "All right. For one night and then we figure
something else out or convince your cook to return."

Soccoro clapped her hands. "*Fabulosa!* Romero's best
cook ever is back in the kitchen. It is a *milagro*."

Adela smiled and shook her head. "A small miracle, maybe, but only for this one night." She followed Soccoro into the kitchen, praying her words would prove to be true. She stopped and looked around after passing through the swinging doors. Nothing about this room appeared to have changed. The renovations had apparently stopped with the dining area and exterior. The appliances and cooking area were all clean and neat, but...almost ancient. "Um...it's pretty much the same as it was ten years ago." She kept her voice soft and neutral, not wanting to offend Soccoro.

Soccoro gave a small laugh. "Well, we didn't have enough in the budget to renovate the entire restaurant." She waved her hands in the air. "But it's still very workable and...clean."

Adela continued to look at every part of the room. "So you decided to skimp on the kitchen? The heart of the restaurant?"

Sandra huffed beside her. "It's not the area the public sees. We had to make them happy as they pay the bills."

"You'll pick up right where you left off." Soccoro's voice was overly cheerful.

"But...these appliances are older than Fabi." Adela motioned toward the ancient refrigerator in the corner.

"It still works. That's what matters," Sandra said. "But I am sorry it's not your fancy TV kitchen."

"*Está bien, está bien,*" Soccoro nearly crooned the words.

Immediate regret at her criticism hit Adela. She walked over to the fridge and pulled open the door, inspecting the fresh produce to see what she had to work with. The lettuce appeared a bit wilted and none of the condiments were brands she recognized. She'd make do. After all, it was only one night.

"I can wash dishes." Fabi rushed over to the sink and grabbed the industrial sprayer. "That way everyone else can cook or wait tables or take the money." Her wide brown eyes sought Adela's.

"Of course, it's okay. It will be fun, getting acquainted all over again with this kitchen and having you here to help, Fabi. Let's get to work."

TWO HOURS LATER, Adela stirred the meat simmering in one pan. The trickle of customers had turned into more of a steady stream—but still not what they needed. "I'll bet they know Mom is cooking, and she's a famous chef," Fabi's words barely registered over the sound of the dishes clanking in the sink, but Adela heard them and grinned. Her daughter was actually proud of her. What a nice change from the sullen young teen who had traveled with them from Los Angeles.

"I think Romero's has a good reputation, and that's why they're coming, but thank you, Fabi." Adela added a little more spice to the sauce in another pan. She dabbed at the sweat on her forehead with the back of her sleeve. She'd worked in an air-conditioned TV set for so long, she'd forgotten what the rush of a hot kitchen was like. Too bad Soccoro's budget hadn't included air conditioning in the kitchen, along with a few new appliances. She had to admit, though, this old stove and cooktop were the best money could buy when they were purchased, and they were still fantastic to work on. Her feet reminded her that it was still another hour to go before they'd be closing, but she could do this. It was actually fun having her daughter in the kitchen helping as well as the satisfaction of working in a real kitchen again, preparing meals for actual people, not just trying to impress a TV audience.

"Order up." Adela placed the plate of *chalupas* on the open window into the dining room and rang the bell. She sprinkled a little cilantro on top to garnish it and added a little more spice than Soccoro's recipe called for, but her presentations were so...plain. They needed just a little bit of help to brighten them and go that extra step to perfection.

Soccoro popped her head in through the swinging doors. "How's it going in here? Everyone holding up okay?"

"Yes, just like you said...like riding a bicicleta." She grinned at her mother-in-law, happy to see the contented look on Soccoro's face. "I will say that I'm happy it wasn't a super busy night, though."

The contented expression faded, and Soccoro shrugged. "I'm afraid that's pretty much how it is most nights. Steady, but never very busy."

A server peered through the window. "A customer wants to know what you put on top of the chalupas."

Adela glanced up. "A little cilantro garnish with parsley on the side."

The server nodded and disappeared, her face a bit flushed.

Adela turned to Soccoro. "Is there a problem?"

"They aren't used to fancy foods, that's all."

"Cilantro and parsley aren't fancy. The cilantro adds to the flavor, and the parsley gives it a little more color, that's all." She moved back in front of her station and opened the lid on a clear plastic tub. "Where're the tomato and lettuce?"

The food prep cook rushed over, filled both bins, and then hurried away.

Soccoro stood by the door, her face filled with pride and love. Adela shot her a glance and smiled. This had been a good night, indeed.

LATER THAT EVENING, Adela dragged herself from the passenger seat of Soccoro's car after she pulled to a stop in front of her home, a gray two-story with mature landscaping and dark trim. It had been too long since she'd been here—not since Mauricio was still alive. She shook herself once again. This was a new day—or a new night, as it were—and even though she was tired, it was a good tired. She and Fabi had helped Soccoro out of a tough spot, and now they could rest and start over tomorrow.

As they walked into the foyer, memories flooded in, but Adela pushed them to the side. She wouldn't spoil this special summer for Fabi.

"Richie, I'm home!" Soccoro knelt down and opened

her arms as a tan Bichon poodle ran down the hall and jumped into her arms, yipping and licking Soccoro's face. "I'm so sorry we're late. Have you been a good boy? I missed you so much. Look who's here." She stood and presented the small dog to Fabi and Adela.

Fabi reached out and scooped the dog into her arms. "He's darling. We're going to be best friends. I love dogs!"

"My neighbor comes over and takes him for a walk, feeds him, and lets him out when I'm gone, but he always misses me so much. Maybe I should start taking him when I travel." She patted the dog's head. "Let me show you to your rooms." Adela followed her down the hall and waited while Soccoro opened a door. "I hope this will be all right? If you want to trade with Fabi, I'm sure she won't mind. I thought it would give you more privacy here than on the pull-out couch in the TV room." Creases wrinkled her forehead and her lips pressed in to a tight line as she looked past Adela into the room.

Adela stood for a moment taking in what appeared to be a teen boy's room that was frozen in time, including sports trophies, posters on the walls, a bed with the corners tucked in, and memorabilia on a shelf near the window. Mauricio's room where he'd grown up. Adela couldn't believe Soccoro hadn't changed this room at all. Her eyes misted, but she blinked them and turned with a smile. "This will be fine. Thank you."

Soccoro hesitated and then squeezed Adela's arm. "Towels are in the closet right outside the bathroom. It's been a few years since you've been here, so if you need anything at all, please let me know. *Buenas noches*, mija."

As soon as Soccoro left and shut the door behind her, Adela walked around the room, touching the mementos and looking at the photos of Mauricio as a young man proudly holding a soccer trophy with his teammates. A flood of happy memories swamped her. Those were good years, and she was thankful she'd had them. She wouldn't have changed anything other than the accident that took her husband's life way too early. But she had Fabi, and she was a treasure she would forever cherish. She picked up a photo on the nightstand—one of her and Mauricio standing in front of Romero's. This must have been taken a year or so before they married. She wiped a tear from her cheek that she hadn't realized had escaped and then put the photo back on the stand. Time to move on.

She kicked off her shoes, stretched out on the bed, propped the pillows beneath her, and then reached for her phone to check e-mail. Right as she picked it up, it rang, and she jumped. She looked at the screen. Matias. As much as she'd like to let it go to voicemail, she hadn't talked to her manager in a few days. "Hey, Matias, it's late."

"Are you sitting down?" Just like Matias...straight to the point without any intro.

"No. I'm lying down. It's been a long, tiring evening, and I'm beat."

"Well, your evening is taking a turn and going to get a lot better. Ready for this?" His voice had a ringing quality as if he was barely holding in the news. He didn't wait for a reply but rushed on. "I just got off the phone with the execs from Gourmond. They're eyeing you for a new series!"

Adela sat up. "Really?"

"A summer with the world's best chefs. Think of that."

"I'm listening."

His voice rushed on as though she hadn't interrupted. "You'd be traveling to cities all over Europe to work with starred chefs and breaking down their recipes for an American audience."

"Are you serious?" Her heartbeat accelerated, and her breath caught.

"Very serious. And the shooting schedule won't conflict with *Alta Cocina*. You're going to have two shows on Gourmond. This is huge!" She heard what sounded like his palm slapping his desk.

"I'm in. Wow. Good job, Matias." She fell back against her pillows, trying not to start whooping with joy. No sense in disturbing the rest of the household this late at night.

"Perfect! It's a twelve-week shoot. The network needs you in London in about ten days..." She could almost hear him rubbing his hands together in glee.

"Hold it. Wait. You said summer series. As in...this summer? Like, ten days from...now?" Adela sat up again, clutching the phone and waiting for his answer.

"Well, yeah. This summer, of course. We wouldn't be talking about a year from now, would we?"

"We could be. I mean, a lot of shows are scheduled

way in advance. This is super short notice. You know I planned to be in San Antonio the entire summer with my family. Fabi will be devastated. She's looked forward to this all year."

A deep sigh sounded on the other end of the line. "It's only for a little over two months...maybe three if the filming doesn't go as fast as they expect. Fabi should understand. Besides, she's into soccer, right? Think what a trip to Europe would mean to her. She could play with international teams and learn things she'd never learn here in the States."

Adela rolled her eyes even though Matias couldn't see her and tried to curb the extreme frustration rising inside. "Try telling that to my daughter. I missed her championship game, Matias. That was a very big deal. She already thinks I'm the worst mother in the world due to the amount of time I spend on the set."

"Of course, she does, she's thirteen. What teenager thinks their parents can do anything right? You're the parent. You need to make the decision you feel is best — and not just for Fabi, but for you, as well. After all, this is your career we're talking about, and this is a huge opportunity."

Adela adjusted the pillow behind her back, but nothing she did felt comfortable. She needed to end this call so she could think. "I can't accept this job without Fabi being onboard."

"Fine. But the network needs an answer soon. Like, tomorrow. Can you talk to her in the morning and get back to me ASAP?"

"Yeah, I'll talk to her, but as much as I'd love to do this, Matias, I can't make any promises." She clicked off the phone and slid it across the nightstand. It landed right in front of the picture of her and Mauricio in front of Romero's. "What would you do? I wish you were here to talk to Fabi for me."

# Chapter Seven

DAVID PUSHED AWAY FROM HIS DESK at *The Telegram* office, sick of staring at the computer screen and coming up blank on what to write next. He couldn't get Adela's reaction out of his head. She'd been irritated — almost angry at him when he'd bumped into her and her family at Tacos Rápidos. Had his interview really upset her so much? She'd walked away and ignored him as though he were a nobody. It wasn't like they hadn't met before. Sure, it had been years since they'd known each other — not dating or anything, but they'd even worked for a summer together at Romero's, and he'd had a major crush on her. Of course, with that many years between, it wasn't likely she'd remember him. Too bad she didn't realize he was just doing his job and not trying to harass her or make her look bad.

He got up, stretched, and then headed for the coffee machine in the break room. Actually, coffee wasn't going to get his mind going — what he needed was to stretch his legs and get some fresh air. Striding past the receptionist, he lifted his fingers in a quick salute. "I'll be back in fifteen minutes or so, Connie. My brain shut down, and I need to get the blood flowing again."

The dark blonde, petite woman in her late forties

glanced up and smiled. "Stretch for me while you're at it." She tipped her head down and resumed staring at her computer monitor.

David shook his head as he pushed open the heavy glass door that led into *The Telegram* offices. Spending so many hours staring at a computer screen couldn't be good, but what could any of them do when they lived with technology, and it paid the bills? Sometimes he thought his dad was right—they'd all be better off if none of it had been invented and they returned to a simpler way of life.

The heat and humidity hit him as soon as he stepped outside, but it was tolerable today—low humidity and only in the mid-eighties, which was pretty mild for summer in San Antonio. He stopped and scanned the street. *Which direction to go?* The park was only a block away—he'd hung out there as a kid shooting baskets and even playing an occasional game of soccer. He headed that direction, his feet beating a rapid tattoo on the warm sidewalk.

A couple of minutes later, he rounded the corner and spotted the green grass and scattering of oak trees, some of them ancient, with wide-spreading boughs that cast welcome shade. It looked like a group of kids had a soccer game going...definitely not an organized team since they had no uniforms and a couple of the kids looked pretty rag-tag. But from the shouts and laughter, the young teens were all having fun.

He stopped next to a young girl with her dark hair pulled back into a ponytail but didn't get too close. He didn't want to scare her—there were too many people in the world that weren't safe, and he didn't want her to get the wrong idea about him. However, something about this girl seemed familiar. Maybe she attended the same church he did? Trying to study her without being too obvious, he sidled a little closer. No, not church. Had she been featured in *The Telegram*? She had a classic face with well-defined cheekbones and pretty brown eyes. Surely, he'd remember if she had been.

David shook his head and studied the two teams playing. It looked like one of them was struggling to keep up with the other. He glanced at the girl again. "Do you play?"

She shot him a look and then bit her lip.

"Sorry, I didn't mean to bother you. I just thought that one of the teams might be able to use another player. Have you asked to join them?"

She shook her head and scuffed her toe against the grass. "No. I don't know any of them, so I didn't want to ask."

"So you *do* play?" He stayed where he was even though he'd like to see her a little closer and maybe jog his memory on where he'd seen her before.

"Yeah. I love soccer." She gave him a small smile that erased the worried expression she'd been wearing.

"Then you should ask to join them. I'll bet they'd be thrilled." He waved at the field as the ball whizzed past. "You can't be any worse than they are, and if you're better, you might help even things up a bit."

A soft giggle escaped her lips. "Maybe. But I don't want to ask."

MIRALEE FERRELL and KIMBERLY ROSE JOHNSON

David nodded. "Yeah, I get that. Hold on a minute." He walked over to a boy standing on the sidelines who'd been trying to coach the losing team. "Hey, you guys open to having someone else join the game?" He hitched a thumb over his shoulder at the young girl. "She knows how to play if you want any help."

The boy's eyes lit with excitement and what looked like cautious hope. "Sure." He trotted over to the girl and said something David didn't hear.

The girl nodded. Then she shot David a quick smile. "Thanks!" She headed onto the field and took a position.

He waved back. "What's your name?"

"Fabi!"

"Have fun, Fabi, and good luck to your new team." David glanced at his watch. His fifteen minutes were over, and it would be closer to twenty-five by the time he got back to the office, but the shy smile and joy on that girl's face had been worth it even if he couldn't place where he'd seen her before.

# Chapter Eight

SANDRA APPLIED RED LIPSTICK WHILE STANDING at the door looking into the entryway mirror. She pressed her lips together. "Perfect." Her favorite floral sundress and wedge sandals were understated yet made her feel beautiful—she really needed that today. She opened her mouth to cite her normal mantra, but after last night, she didn't have the heart.

"Let me see you, *Niña*." Abuela stood behind her.

She turned. "What do you think?"

"You are lovely."

"It doesn't look like I tried too hard does it?"

Abuela tsked. "You are a natural beauty." She cupped Sandra's cheek with the palm of her hand. "If he doesn't treat you like a princess, then you forget about him."

Sandra grinned. "I thought you wanted to marry me off?"

"Only to the right man. There are plenty more men out there. I want you to find the kind of love that lasts a lifetime."

"Does that even exist anymore?" Half the people she knew were divorced or in and out of relationships regularly. Another reason to keep her focus on work.

Sadness filled Abuela's eyes. "Yes, mi amor. Have faith. Now scoot before you're late."

"I'm going." Sandra shouldered her purse and fled out the door. Anthony offered to pick her up, but if the date was a bust like every other one her grandmother had set her up on, she wanted to be able to avoid the awkward car ride home.

Thankfully, traffic was light for once, and she found a parking spot near Nola. She'd heard about the New Orleans-inspired restaurant and had checked out their menu online. It was nothing like Romero's, which would be a nice treat.

A clean shaven, dark-haired man around five foot ten strode toward her. He raised a hand in greeting. "Sandra?"

"Anthony?" She liked what she saw but would reserve judgment. More than once, she'd learned the hard way to not judge a person by their appearance. At least she wasn't taller than him, even with her wedges.

"Yes." He held his hand toward her. "It's nice to meet you."

She grasped his firm handshake—no spark. "You too." She smiled politely. Okay, so no spark from his touch didn't mean this date would be a flop. "I'm starving." She nodded toward the house with patio dining in front.

"I like a woman with a good appetite." He flashed perfect white teeth. "I made reservations. We're late, so hopefully, they held our table." He motioned toward the entrance. "Shall we?"

She was only five minutes late. From her experience, their table was probably being prepared right now. "I saw online they serve *beignets*. I've always wanted to try one."

"You've never had a beignet?"

She shook her head as he opened the door for her. "Thank you." She walked inside and breathed in the mix of Cajun and Mexican scents. Her stomach growled.

A few minutes later, they were seated outside on the patio. She left the menu on the table.

Anthony raised a brow. "You already know what you're going to order?"

She nodded. "Chicken and beignets. Completely opposite from my normal fare." Her mouth watered just thinking about the food. If it was half as good as she'd read online, then they were both in for a treat.

"My grandmother mentioned you work at a Mexican diner."

She sat taller and raised her chin slightly. "I'm the assistant manager at Romero's."

He nodded as he studied the menu. "What do you want to do with your life?"

"I'm doing it." She met his gaze when he lowered the menu. "Someday, I want to take over running the restaurant from my aunt."

"Oh, it's a family business. Now I get why that's all you want to do."

She narrowed her eyes. "What is that supposed to mean?"

He placed the menu on the table. "I didn't mean any offense."

"Then explain yourself, because it sounded like you think managing a restaurant is an inferior job." *All she wanted to do?* Running a restaurant was a full-time job. A career. One she looked forward to every day.

"I didn't mean that at all. You chose a difficult profession with little reward."

"What are you talking about?" She never should've been sucked in by his deep voice. She found her job rewarding most of the time. Though recently, not quite so much. With Adela here to rub Sandra's nose in her success, she wasn't too crazy about her job, but Adela would leave soon.

"You aren't helping people or changing the course of someone's life."

Anger burned through her. "I see. Providing an enjoyable meal experience with tasty food is not helping people? There are a lot of people who would disagree with you." Pretty much every customer that walked into Romero's for starters.

A young and perky waitress flounced to their table. "I'm Stephanie. May I take your order?"

Sandra smiled sweetly. "I'd like the chicken and beignets to go."

Stephanie's pen stopped moving, and she looked up. "To go?"

"Yes." She smiled sweetly at Anthony, although she'd much rather have glared. Clearly, this date was a disaster, but she would not leave without food.

"Okay. What would you like, sir?"

"Avocado tostada for *here*." He shot Sandra a look of defiance.

"Should I bring an extra plate to split the meal?" Stephanie asked.

"That won't be necessary." Sandra smiled sweetly. "We'll need separate checks too."

Stephanie collected their menus, turned, and walked away.

"You're leaving?" Frown lines littered Anthony's forehead.

"My grandmother likes to set me up on blind dates. So far she's O for ten."

"Kind of sounds like you might be the one with the problem."

She clenched her hands in her lap. "Perhaps, expecting a man to value me as a human and not belittle my chosen profession is asking too much?" She shrugged. "Call me picky, but I'd rather be alone for the rest of my life than be treated as less than."

His face reddened. He looked down and then back at her. "I was told you were a career woman. I assumed you were a professional like me."

"I might not be an attorney or work in a business office, but I am a professional. The bills don't pay themselves." Well, maybe a few get withdrawn automatically, but that was beside the point. "Without me, my aunt would never be able to have the freedom to leave town and do what she wants."

"So...you work for your family."

She bristled but held herself in check. "And that's a problem because...?"

"You didn't earn it. Nepotism is how you got where you are."

MIRALEE FERRELL and KIMBERLY ROSE JOHNSON

"If I was the assistant manager here, you would show some respect?" She highly doubted this man knew the meaning of the word. No, that wasn't fair. He had been a gentleman up until they'd started talking about her career choice. What was it with this guy? She'd never met anyone who looked down on her position at Romero's.

"It's still not the kind of professional career I was led to believe you were in, but yes. You would have earned the right to be assistant manager."

She rolled her eyes. "How about we sit here quietly until the food arrives? I'll pay for my meal, we'll tell our grandmothers it didn't work out, and we'll never see one another again?"

"I guess. Though I was really looking forward to getting to know you."

"Why?" She couldn't figure out this guy.

"I've heard nice things about you."

Her ire melted a little. "Such as?"

"You are a college graduate with a head for business."

She blinked. "You are a very confusing man. You knew my qualifications and yet you still insulted not only my career choice but the fact I chose to help my family. What gives? What am I missing?"

"I guess, I expected more."

Their waitress approached wearing a wide smile. "Here you go." She handed a to-go box to Sandra with her bill taped to the top and then placed a plate filled with amazing looking food in front of Anthony.

"Thank you." Sandra handed her a twenty. "Keep the change."

"Thanks." Stephanie pocketed the cash and went to another table.

Sandra stood. "I wish I could say it was nice meeting you, but I don't lie." She strutted to her pickup, climbed in, and closed the door. Where should she go? The scent of the food beside her called to her, and she remembered how hungry she was. One thing was certain, she would not sit here and eat. She started the engine and then drove, not paying particular attention to where she was going.

Sandra finally pulled into Romero's parking lot and killed the engine. It figured she would end up here. She probably shouldn't go home yet, and since this place was her second home, it made sense she'd come here without thinking. Though now that Tía Soccoro was back and Manny had quit, being here didn't give her the warm and comfy feeling she craved right now.

Sandra lowered the windows on her pickup and reached for the box of food. Hopefully, it would still taste good after sitting in the box for thirty minutes. She bit into a beignet and grinned. "Now this is what I call worth the trouble."

"What's worth the trouble?" a man asked.

She whipped her head toward the window. "Victor! You scared the daylights out of me. What are you doing here?" Victor Rodrigues owned and managed a Mexican food truck that frequented the neighborhood, though she wished he'd find a new location as it cut into their bottom line.

"I was about to ask you the same question. I thought

you went to church on Sunday mornings?" His dark brows rose in question.

Fear shot through her. "Are you stalking me?"

"Hardly. We go to the same church. I usually sit in the balcony."

That she never saw him made sense, but it was unsettling to know he saw her and she hadn't noticed him, assuming he spoke the truth. "Why aren't you there now?"

"Overslept and thought I'd get a jumpstart on food prep."

"You should take Sunday's off." She didn't understand why he wouldn't give himself a day off, but she admired his work ethic.

He raised a brow. "Perhaps I should." He tilted his head to the side. "Is everything okay?"

"Yes. I'm going to go to the late service today." She waved the beignet in front of her face before taking another delectable bite.

Victor chuckled. "You must have gone to Nola. You were smart to go early. What'd you think?"

"So good, but my date was a bust." The thought of Anthony made her blood run hot. The man was infuriating. She pushed him out of her mind and focused on Victor.

He frowned. "You had a date this morning?"

"Brunch."

His face cleared. "I never thought of that. Cool. Not so good though, huh?"

She raised a shoulder. "I've had worse, but no, it wasn't good."

"I'm sorry." He seemed to really mean it.

"Thank you." She'd never realized he had a sweet side. She'd only witnessed the hardworking food-truck-owner side to him. She leaned forward and looked out the windshield. "I don't see your truck."

"I was driving by and spotted you sitting here. I parked around the corner in my usual spot but wanted to make sure you were okay."

Her jaw dropped, and she quickly snapped it closed. Okay, Victor was a seriously nice guy. "Wow. You don't happen to be looking for a job, do you?" As if he had time, but maybe he was looking for a change.

He chuckled. "I'm kind of busy with my business. Not sure how I'd cook at both places."

"I figured but had to ask. Business is going well then? Wait, how'd you know we need a new cook?"

"Manny stopped in to see if we were hiring last night."

"No! Did you hire him?" What happened to loyalty? She should have known Manny didn't know the meaning of the word. He went to their biggest competitor the same day he'd left Romero's.

"Told him to fill out an application, but I'm not hiring."

*Whew!* If Manny found another job, he would never return to Romero's. Though after that stunt she didn't want him back. That still left them without a head cook. Adela couldn't moonlight as their chef indefinitely. She had a life, and it wasn't in San Antonio, thank goodness. Sandra would never measure up to Tía Soccoro's expectations with Adela around. The woman was too talented and perfect—at least her aunt seemed to think so.

A text lit her phone. "It's my grandmother." She held up her phone.

*How's it going?*

Victor nodded. "Okay. Well, I'm sorry about your date. Better luck next time."

She shook her head. "Nu-uh. No way. No. More. Blind. Dates. Thanks again for checking on me." She noted the untouched beignet and reached for it. "Do you want the other beignet? I can't eat all this food." She picked it up with a napkin and handed it to him.

His face lit. His brown eyes sparkled in the late morning sunshine. "Thanks."

She caught her breath and shook her head. What was she thinking? She could not fall for her biggest competitor. Her phone vibrated again. Abuela. "I should probably give her a call."

"Right. See you." He waved and strode toward the sidewalk.

She pressed in Abuela's number.

"You didn't have to call me," Grandma said. "But since you did, how's it going?"

"It's not. He was insulting. He said nepotism was the only reason I had the assistant manager job at Romero's. Can you believe that?"

"I'm sorry, mi amor."

"No more blind dates. Okay? I need a break. Promise?"

"I can't promise that, but I will be pickier. I reserve the right to set you up with the perfect man."

"That's not how this works." She stifled a laugh. What was she going to do with her grandmother? The woman was obsessed with marrying her off.

"When are you coming home? There's still time to get to church on time."

"Soon. Be ready and waiting." She disconnected the call and then reached for the box and quickly ate the chicken. It was almost as good as the beignet. Maybe she should have stuck out the date after all. No. Leaving was the right thing to do. Maybe her action would keep another woman from the same fate. Anthony was clearly an intelligent man. Hopefully, he wouldn't demean his next date.

She wiped her fingers and headed home. Abuela would be furious if they were late to church once again because of her. Today, they'd be early for a change.

A short while later she pulled into the driveway.

Abuela charged out the door, looking as youthful as a teenager in her turquoise dress and sandals. Her long silver hair flowed to her shoulders. Apparently, her grandmother had more energy than Sandra did today.

Grandma opened the passenger door and climbed inside. "I wish you'd trade this beast in for a sensible car."

Sandra resisted rolling her eyes. "You look nice in that dress."

"This old thing?"

Sandra backed out of the driveway. "You taught me to say thank you when someone gives a compliment."

*"Gracias."* Though when Abuela said the word, it was spoken begrudgingly. "It's your week to clean the house. I noticed crumbs on the kitchen counter and the floor needs to be mopped."

Sandra winced. "I did clean the house. I must have missed a few crumbs." She wouldn't mention the crumbs had to have fallen this morning while she was gone since Abuela had cleaned last night.

"And the floor." Grandmother crossed her arms.

"Right. I'll get to it."

"Humph."

Sandra glanced at her grandmother. "Are you okay? You seem to be bothered about something." Abuela was always testy about her home being clean, but this attack felt motived by something else.

"I spoke with Anthony's grandma after your call. She said her grandson called you a high maintenance diva who expected the world to serve her every whim."

Sandra gasped.

"How will you ever find a husband with a reputation like that?"

"You know me, Abuela. He's angry because I left our date." She glanced toward her grandmother. Why would she believe a stranger's lies over her own granddaughter?

"Apparently I don't know you as well as I thought."

Sandra pulled into the church parking lot. They were late. Again.

Grandma slid out and strode toward the church building.

Sandra followed slowly. Hopefully, this morning wasn't a sign of the week to come because much more of this, and she'd take Mya up on her standing offer to be roomies. She loved her abuela, but sometimes she was a lot to bear.

# Chapter Nine

ADELA MOVED THE PAN OF SIMMERING meat on the stove to the side and turned off the heat. She'd have to face her daughter and mother-in-law in a matter of minutes, and she still wasn't sure how she was going to share Matias's news. The last thing she wanted was to disappoint Fabi again. Maybe fixing her daughter's favorite breakfast would help, although she could envision the disappointment on Soccoro's face as well. Why did life have to be so difficult?

Adela would have happily stayed in her pajamas snuggled under the covers, but she hadn't slept much since the call last night, and she needed to get this chore over with—after all, she had promised Matias to give him an answer today.

Soccoro breezed into the kitchen, makeup, hair, and clothing picture perfect as usual, even this early on a Sunday morning. Richie trotted along at her heels but stopped to sniff his food dish. "Just a moment, my baby. I'll feed you before we eat." As she removed the dry and wet food from their respective containers, she eyed Adela. "*Qué pasa*? I was going to cook you breakfast this morning. You must have gotten up very early to have this nearly done. What's going on?"

Fabi walked slowly into the room, giving Adela a slight reprieve on answering. "Good morning, Fabi. Did you sleep well?"

Her daughter gave a soft grunt and slid into her seat. She'd never been much of a morning person. It was amazing she'd even gotten up in time for breakfast since it was summer and no school. "I smelled something cooking, so I got up." She raised bleary eyes to her mother.

Adela plated the dishes and set them in the center of the table. "Your favorites...*Agua de Jamaica, chilaquiles, huevos rancheros...*"

Fabi's expression sharpened, and she narrowed her eyes. "Why? What's up?"

Adela bit her lip and then managed a smile. "To celebrate summer and being here in San Antonio. Enjoy!" She slid into her place and waited for Fabi and Soccoro to load their plates and start eating before she took a small helping. Her stomach felt a bit queasy at the moment, and she wasn't sure she cared to eat, but she had to keep up appearances. She waited until they'd eaten several bites. Then she took a big breath and let it out slowly. "So...I have a bit of news. Exciting news, I think." She looked from one to the other and waited.

Fabi dabbed at her mouth with a napkin, a definite sparkle lighting her eyes. "We're going to Six Flags?"

Soccoro nodded. "Sí. Good idea, mija. That would be fun, but we'll have to find a time when we all can go. You know, maybe a day when Romero's is closed. Mondays are usually good times to get away."

Adela's heart sank. "Um. Yeah. I mean, no. I'm sure

we can go to Six Flags at some point, but that's not what I wanted to share. I got a call from Matias last night with amazing news. He said the network wants me to host another TV show—a new one. Isn't that amazing?"

"Congratulations! That's wonderful, Adela." Soccoro put her fork down and reached over to pat Adela's hand.

"Wow, Mom. Cool!" Fabi grinned at her. "But how will you do that and your regular show?" Her grin faded. "That means I'm not going to see you even half as much as I did last school year if you're trying to do two shows."

"No, that won't be a problem. I'll only be shooting my regular one when you go back to school. This...well, um...it's in Europe." She pushed the words out fast, hoping somehow that would help with what she had to say. "I'll get to work with some of the worlds' best chefs, and you and I will get to spend the entire summer in Europe. There will be time to explore and for you to make new friends and maybe even get on a top soccer team while we're there. Won't that be fun?"

Fabi just stared at Adela, her eyes wide. "But...we were supposed to spend the summer here, in San Antonio, with Abuela."

"I know, but sometimes things change. You could even go to a world-class soccer camp if you want. Wouldn't that be amazing? It's something we've talked about in the past. And this is a huge opportunity for my career. You understand that, right?"

Fabi continued to stare without saying a word. Finally, she pushed back her chair, tossed her napkin on top of her half-finished meal, rose, and stalked from the room.

Soccoro looked at Adela with raised brows and gave a small shake of her head.

Adela gazed from her to the door where Fabi had disappeared. "Fabi. Wait. We need to talk."

ADELA FOLLOWED FABI in to the living room and got there in time to see her daughter flop onto the plush, high-backed couch, grab a pillow, and hug it to her chest. "Fabi, I'm sorry I took you by surprise, but you know what kind of job I have. This is my career. I can't just ignore it when my agent wants to line up something new for me that will help advance it. I know this isn't what we planned, but we can try to make the best of it."

Fabi clutched the pillow even tighter and buried her face in the brown fabric. "It's always work." Her words came out muffled but clear enough to understand. She raised her head and glared, but Adela saw a sheen of tears in her eyes. "You never stop working. We've been planning this trip all year, and I thought maybe...maybe this summer would be different. We haven't been back to San Antonio since Dad died." She swiped at the tears and turned her head away.

Adela sank into the easy chair across from the couch, closed her eyes for a moment, and then shot up a quick prayer for help. "I didn't give Matias an answer yet. I told him I'd talk to you, that I wanted us to make this decision together."

"Good." Fabi's gaze drilled into her own. "Then I say no. I don't want to go. I want to stay here."

She shifted in her seat, not sure how to respond. She had said they'd decide together—but did that mean she needed to turn Matias down if Fabi didn't change her mind? Could she really do that and sabotage her career? "But, Fabi, it's Europe. We've never been there. Think of all the wonderful places we could visit together. The memories we'd build."

"I don't care. I want to stay here and build memories. I don't care about Europe. This is home, and I want to stay home." Fabi tilted her chin in the stubborn, determined look that Adela recognized as one of her own.

"When I was your age, all I wanted to do was get out of San Antonio and see the world. The last thing I wanted was to get trapped here."

"Well I'm not you." Fabi stood, reached into her backpack at the end of the couch, and extracted her soccer ball.

Adela sat up. "Where are you going?"

"To the park. I don't have to go to Europe to play soccer." She headed to the door, and the quiet click of the latch thundered more than if she'd slammed it.

Adela walked without much thought back to the kitchen, almost surprised to see Soccoro sitting quietly at the table as though waiting for the verdict. "She doesn't want to go to Europe." Adela slid into a chair, picked up her glass of orange juice, and then set it back down.

Soccoro took a drink of her coffee. "I'm not surprised. She's been looking forward to this trip all year."

"Maybe she'll come around. Let's both talk to her, right? After all, I don't have to leave for another ten days." Adela picked up her fork and pushed her leftover food around on her plate.

Soccoro didn't speak.

Adela looked up,

Soccoro raised her brows. "What if you turned down the job?"

"Not you too!" Adela sat back hard against her chair. "This is my career. It's what I do. I can't just walk away from an opportunity like this. It might never come again."

Soccoro took another sip from her mug. "Never mind. I'm sure you know what you're doing and what is best for your daughter."

"It's a big opportunity, Soccoro." Adela sighed. "My own international cooking show. I could be the Latina Anthony Bourdain! I honestly never dreamed I'd get this kind of a chance."

"You can try to talk to her, but I doubt Fabi will change her decision. When she puts her mind to something, she's as stubborn as both of us put together."

Adela sighed and took a bite of her breakfast, but somehow, she'd lost her appetite. She'd known Fabi wouldn't be overjoyed with this new job offer, but she'd hoped she might be cajoled into at least considering it. What teen wouldn't be excited about Europe? She tried to put on a smile and raised her gaze to Soccoro. Maybe it was time to change the subject. "Did you ever hear from Manny? Do you think there's any chance he'll come back and cook for you again?"

"I did. I called him and did everything short of begging. He said he's not going to come back. I don't know if giving him a bigger salary would help at this point, and I'm afraid it would have to be way higher than anything I can afford."

Adela placed her fork back on her plate. "What are you going to do?"

"I'm not sure yet. At least we're closed today, but I need to find someone fast. Maybe I'll check with the unemployment office." She shrugged and raised her hands in the air. "I don't know. I'll figure it out. I always do."

"I can help out for another day or two. It's not like the new job starts this week. That would give you a little more time to find someone who's suitable and not feel rushed." It was the least she could do. She wanted to make someone in this family happy, and it didn't look like she was going to have any luck with Fabi on that score.

Soccoro dabbed at her lips with a napkin. "I can't ask you to do that. This is supposed to be your vacation." She raised one brow. "Besides, you'll be leaving soon, and you probably should do a few fun things with Fabi before you go."

"I kind of enjoyed being back in the kitchen. Fabi seemed like she did too. Maybe we should see if she wants to help for a day or two? Make it a family project."

A slow smile spread across Abuela's face. "A few more days in San Antonio, and you'll forget all about Europe, sí?"

Adela rolled her eyes.

Soccoro picked up her plate and took it to the sink. "I need to do a little grocery shopping. Want to come along?"

"Sure." Adela took the plate Soccoro handed her and placed it in the dishwasher. "But let's change it up a bit this week."

"Change what up?" Soccoro straightened and stared at her.

"Let's buy all the fruits and veggies local. They are so much fresher and better. I'm sure there are a few farmer's markets within driving distance, right?"

"Maybe. But they are too expensive. I shop at the discount grocery stores."

Adela winced. "Where they often sell three-or-four-day old produce. If not older."

Soccoro gave her head a hard shake. "No. I can't afford to buy there."

"I'll buy the food this week. I need to help out more anyway. You're paying for everything here, so I'll buy the fresh produce for the restaurant."

"That is out of the question!" Soccoro planted her hands on her hips.

"But I want to show you what a difference really fresh produce can make. Please, Soccoro? Just let me do it this once?"

"Adela..."

"You said business hasn't been great." She jumped in before Soccoro could change her mind...indecision warred in her mother-in-law's face. "If the renovations didn't make much difference, maybe trying a better-quality produce will. Don't you want to at least try?"

Adela scowled. Then her face softened. "Maybe...I don't know. Just because something is more expensive, it doesn't mean it's better."

Adela grinned and pulled her into a hug. "You won't be sorry. I'm paying this time, so don't bother to even bring your purse. Come on. We'll pick up Fabi on the way. This is going to be fun!"

# Chapter Ten

DAVID PARKED HIS CAR AT HIS favorite farmer's market. They sold the best watermelons in San Antonio, and his mouth watered at the thought all the way here. It was nice to have a day off. He felt as if all he did anymore was work, yet it didn't quite hold the same joy it did a few years ago. He shut his car door and turned to face the large striped tent that covered at least two dozen tables loaded with every fresh fruit and vegetable a person could ever want. Large signs hung from the edges proclaiming fresh, juicy melons, fresh salsa, homemade jams, and more. He was going to load up today and eat healthy for the next week. He almost rubbed his hands together in anticipation.

He wandered over to the watermelons, picked up one, held it on his shoulder close to his ear, and gave it a couple of light thumps. A deep—but not too deep—sound resonated, and he smiled. It didn't sound flat or overripe. Just perfect. This was the one. Walking over to a cart, he pulled it out of the lineup and wheeled it back to the melons, only the first thing that would go in his cart today.

A sweet voice that sounded familiar came from a few tables over, and he raised his head to see if he could spot who it belonged to. A woman with collar-length blond hair and wearing a flowing red-and-white striped shirt stood with her back to him as she talked to someone just out of sight. "This is all so amazing. Look at all the rich colors." She waved her hand at the stack of tomatoes and then held up one. "It's perfect. It even smells ripe." She handed it to the woman just out of sight. "Can't you tell a difference?"

She pointed at the table closer to him. "Look. They have samples." She reached out and grabbed the hand of what appeared to be a young teen. "Come on, Fabi. Soccoro. Let's try them."

A soft smile creased David's face. Adela. Then he spotted the girl she held by the hand. That was the same girl he'd met at the soccer game. Was she a relative? Maybe one of Soccoro's granddaughters?

Adela picked up a toothpick, plunged it into a chunk of cantaloupe, and then popped it into her mouth. She closed her eyes for a moment. "Hmm. Perfect. Try one, Fabi." She grabbed a fresh toothpick, selected a melon, and held it out.

The teen took a step back. "Mom. I'm not a baby. I don't need you to feed me." She crossed her arms, huffed, and then watched Soccoro try one. "Are they good, Abuela?"

"Sí. Not too bad, I guess." Soccoro held out a toothpick with a melon piece on it to the girl. "Here. See what you think."

He smiled as the girl took the melon without a word of complaint about her grandmother feeding her.

"It's good! Let's take a couple of these home."

Adela nudged Soccoro. "See. I told you so. You like them too, right?"

The older woman shrugged. "I suppose. Although I've had better." She lifted her head and sniffed. "I still don't think we need to buy things here for Romero's."

"Soccoro." Adela narrowed her eyes and appeared to pretend to glare.

"All right." Soccoro waved her hands in the air. "Está bien. They are good. But maybe our customers won't like these changes."

"They will recognize good food when it's served to them. I guarantee it. After all, I am Romero's top chef, so what I say goes."

Soccoro chuckled and shook her head.

Adela placed three cantaloupes in her basket, and David turned away. He shouldn't be standing here spying on this family, but it did his heart good to see them smiling and enjoying their day. He missed his family, and this short peek into Adela's warmed him while it also gave him a pang of longing for something more. He'd better get his own shopping done and head home. He couldn't stand around doing nothing all day. Grabbing a few other items without really even thinking, he headed to the checkout stand. Maybe a jar of that amazing strawberry jam would go well on his toast in the morning. He parked his cart to the side and stepped over to the table housing the jam, took two, placed them in his cart, and then steered back toward the cash register.

He stopped a few paces away. Adela had gotten there first, and she handed the cashier her credit card as he placed the last item in what looked to be the third bag, all bursting with produce. She tucked the card back in her purse, shifted it on her shoulder, reached for one bag, and then pulled a second one toward her. David glanced around wondering where Soccoro and Adela's daughter had gotten to. No way could she handle all three of those bags. He stepped forward. "Would you like a hand with those, miss?" He tried not to grin as she turned around, her expression warm and smiling.

"Yes, gracias!" She stared at him, and her smile faded. "Oh. It's you."

"Remember, the name is David? You have your hands full. Would you like help or not?" He cocked his head to the side and kept his smile in place.

"No, thanks. I can get it." She reached for the third bag, pulled it toward her, and then tried to lift all three of them at the same time, wedging one in between the other two. The stubborn woman was going to drop them all and bruise the fruit if she wasn't careful.

ADELA GLANCED AT David. Yeah. David. The man with the annoying smirk waiting for her to reply. She sighed and set them back down. "Fine. I suppose I do need help since there are people waiting behind me, and all the employees here appear to be busy." She looked around the tent. "And I have no idea where my daughter and Soccoro went."

He waved a hand at one of the bags. "What's all this? A light snack?"

*Infuriating man.* "If you must know, it's for my mother-in-law's restaurant. I'm helping her shop."

"Romero's?" He crossed his arms and tipped his head to the side.

She started and blinked a couple of times. "You're familiar with her restaurant?"

"Of course. I go there regularly."

She tried not to roll her eyes. "Really. You?"

He smirked again. "What, you think I never eat out?"

"Of course not. It's a great place to eat. But it's not fancy, and I assumed that's the type of place you'd frequent." She held up one hand. "I mean, it's a great place to eat, and it has marvelous food. I love it."

He shrugged and then reached for a bag. "I stop in at Romero's at least once a week. Sometimes more. Soccoro serves the type of food I can really get into. You thought I was pertinacious, didn't you?"

Adela stifled a laugh. "I haven't thought of you one way or the other."

"Ha. Good one. But I doubt that's true." He shifted the bag to his hip and reached for a second one. "I'll get this, and you take the third. Lead the way, fair lady." He shot her a killer smile.

Her heart skipped a beat, and she almost ground her teeth in frustration. She was not attracted to this man nor would she ever be. Time to get back on safe ground. "Do you have any recommendations, or places to stay away from while I'm in town? After all, you are a renowned food critic." The words came out a bit more sarcastic than she'd planned, and she wished she could take them back.

He cocked one brow at her. "Yeah. Stay away from my friend Julio's agua fresca stand. I'd recommend you definitely don't go there."

This time Adela laughed out loud. "I'll be sure to stop by there soon."

"Especially when you consider how mild the summer weather is here. Nothing like not having a cool, refreshing *agua de melon* right about now..."

Adela's gaze followed his to the blistering sun pouring down as they stepped out from under the tent that had created welcome shade. "Ugh. I'm beginning to hate you."

David gave her that annoying smirk again, but this time, it was tinged with a bit of a smile that sent her heart fluttering.

"Now I want one." She reached into her pocket, pulled out her key fob, and popped the trunk.

He followed her lead and deposited the groceries inside and then stood. "You won't regret it—especially since Julio is one of your biggest fans."

"Lead the way. Apparently, Soccoro and Fabi are still browsing, but since it's right across the street, I'll see them when they come out and can wave at them to join us."

DAVID LED THE way to the stand, the blood surging through his veins as the gorgeous blonde strode along beside him. It was apparent she didn't remember him from their teen years—a lot of time had passed and they'd both lived what felt like a lifetime since then—but he'd never quite forgotten his first crush. "Julio, look who I found."

His friend, a man about the same age as he was in his mid-thirties, spun around and nearly dropped a cantaloupe as his gaze fell on Adela. "Adela Romero! *Dios mío.* I thought David was joking when he said he saw you yesterday. What are you doing here in San Antonio?"

"I'm visiting my family."

Julio glanced from David to Adela and then back to David and narrowed his eyes. "I can't believe you're hanging out with him after the way he went after you in that interview."

David drew in a short breath and glanced at Adela. He'd been hoping that wouldn't come up again anytime soon, but maybe it was just as well.

Adela threw him a look that didn't bode well for him and then turned her attention back to Julio. "You saw it?"

"Yeah. Me and everyone else in San Antonio."

She winced. *"Fantástico."*

David shook his head. "It wasn't that bad. You may have gotten a little heated, but I think overall it was a solid interview."

"Ha! For you, maybe. Certainly not for me."

Julio waved an expressive hand. "An agua melon is gonna make all your troubles go away, I promise. I source the fruit from my sister's husband. He owns an organic farm outside the city. Want to try one?"

"Sure. Anything cold and wet sounds fabuloso right

now." Adela gave Julio a smile that should have melted his heart—it certainly would have David's if she'd only aimed it his way.

Julio handed her a cup and appeared to wait with his breath held until she took her first sip. "You like it? It's good, yes?"

Adela's face lit with pure pleasure. "It's amazing. The flavors are so bright and crisp. I'd love to drink this all day, and I wouldn't get tired of it."

Julio lit up like a Christmas tree in July. "David, Pinch me. *Pellízcame.* I must be dreaming. Adela, the fabulosa cook likes it!"

David reached over and pinched Julio. He couldn't resist, and he followed it with a grin.

"Ouch." Julio scowled in mock pain.

David threw back his head and laughed. "You asked for it, my friend."

"So I did." Julio rubbed his arm.

Adela reached into her purse and pulled out a twenty. "How much do I owe you?"

Julio drew back, his eyes wide and hands raised. "You owe me nothing! It was an honor to serve you, and you made me a happy man with your praise."

David shoved a five into Julio's hand. "My treat." He smiled at Adela, hoping she'd understand his next words. "Consider it an apology."

Her brows puckered, and she opened her lips, but a shout from across the street interrupted. She turned and waved. "Soccoro. Fabi. Are you ready to go?"

"Sí. We'll head to the car." Soccoro waved in return

and then pointed at the car parked on the curb. She gazed from David to Adela. "Don't rush on our account."

Warm color rose in Adela's cheeks, and she shook her head. "I'm ready now." She turned to Julio. "Thank you for the wonderful drink." She bit her lip and glanced at David, her cheeks getting even a little rosier. "And thank you for buying it for me. I need to run."

David gave her a warm smile, loving that she appeared a bit flustered as she'd glanced at him. "See you around?"

ADELA DASHED ACROSS the street, trying to forget David's question as she'd left his side. She shouldn't have been rude. She should have replied, but he'd really thrown her when he'd paid for the drink, apologized, and then asked if he'd see her again. Sure, it was a common enough question that typically didn't mean anything, but something in his tone told her otherwise. Did she want him to mean more or maybe even see him again? Right now, she'd better switch her attention to Soccoro and Fabi. Either one of them were discerning enough to start asking questions if she wasn't careful.

She jogged across the street, squelching the desire to look over her shoulder to see if David was watching. Plastering on a wide smile for Soccoro's benefit, she stopped at the car. "Sorry for not seeing you come out. I ran into that guy again from Tacos Rápidos."

Soccoro nodded absentmindedly. "I'm happy you're making friends, but we must get this overpriced food into the refrigerator before it goes bad. Hurry, girls. Get in the car, and let's get these to Romero's. *¡Ándale!*"

Adela sucked in a shallow breath, blew it out in relief, and then turned to face her daughter.

Fabi stood there, arms crossed and brows raised, a slight smirk tugging at her lips. "A new friend, huh, Mom? Interesting." She slipped into the backseat before Adela could reply, but not before she saw the distinct twinkle in her daughter's brown eyes.

# Chapter Eleven

SANDRA SET THE MOP IN THE bucket and stepped back to admire the clean entryway. Abuela would not find one reason to pick at her housekeeping skills now. She'd made sure the kitchen sparkled and even washed the inside of the windows. Not how she had planned to spend her Sunday afternoon, but if she were honest, cleaning was relaxing and helped ease her stress. Today had certainly held more stress than she'd anticipated.

"Abuela, I just finished mopping. Be careful if you get up."

"Sí, gracias. Come talk to me."

Sandra stepped carefully to a rug and then to another until she reached the sofa and dropped down to snuggle into the soft cushions.

"You work too hard." Abuela kept her focus on the blanket she was crocheting.

Hadn't she berated her before church for not cleaning well enough? It seemed no matter what she did it was wrong. "I enjoy cleaning."

"Pff. No one enjoys cleaning."

"I guess I'm the exception." She didn't care to argue.

"I spoke with Anthony's grandmother after church and informed her of how rude her grandson had been to you. She was mortified. I had been so taken aback by her attack on your character that I'd neglected to share with her what you had told me on the phone. That should squash any rumors about you being high maintenance."

Did people seriously have time to gossip about her? Sandra couldn't imagine that was the case. "Thank you for sticking up for me, but it would be best if you let me find my own dates from now on."

"I would, but you never date."

"Maybe that's because I've not been given a chance. When my life is already filled with blind dates and work, how am I supposed to meet a man I might be interested in?" And that was a big *might*. So far, the only man she knew that she cared to spend more than a few minutes with was Victor, and he was out of the question.

Abuela set her crocheting aside. "I'll make a deal with you."

*This ought to be interesting.*

"What?"

"You schedule your own dates for one month with a minimum of one date a week, and I promise to not set you up on a blind date."

"Deal!" Ack what had she done? If she didn't follow through, there was no doubt Abuela would return to her matchmaking with even more vigor.

Abuela waved a finger at her. "You go even one week without a date on the calendar and I'll resume my search."

Sandra sighed. "Fine. But for the record, I'm not husband hunting."

"We'll see." A smug smile rested on grandmother's face.

Sandra stood. "I'll be in my room." She needed to call Mya for advice. This was her big chance to finally get her grandmother to leave her love life alone, and she couldn't mess it up.

She closed and locked her bedroom door and called Mya.

"Hey, what's up? It's not like you to call. You usually text."

"I know, but this is too big for a text. Actually, this is a conversation to have in person. Do you have time to meet somewhere?"

"Even if I didn't, I'd say yes. You have me very curious. There's a park with plenty of shade near my apartment. Want to meet there?"

"I remember it. I'll text when I get there if I don't see you." The cutoffs and tank top she'd cleaned in would have to do. She didn't want to waste time changing. Though tempted to sneak out her window, she wasn't a teen. She was a grown woman who could come and go as she pleased.

She penned a note on a piece of paper, slipped out of her bedroom, and then tiptoed to the door. She placed the note to her grandmother on the console table and left, closing and locking the door softly behind her. Guilt knotted her stomach. Maybe she was being immature, but she didn't want to encounter her grandmother right now.

A half hour later, she parked and strolled over to where Mya sat on a park bench in the shade. "Thanks for meeting me." She hugged Mya and then sat beside her. "I need your help. My grandmother and I made a deal. She'll stop setting me up on blind dates if I find one on my own for at least one night each week for the next four weeks."

"Wow! What're you going to do? If you don't find dates, you know she's going to be worse than before."

"I know." Sandra bit down on her bottom lip. Making that deal sounded good in the moment, but if she failed... "Do you have any suggestions?"

"You and I could go out one week. She'd never know it wasn't really a date."

"I won't lie to her. I need to follow the rules or accept defeat."

Mya blew out her breath in a huff. "Okay. What do you want to do? There are lots of dating apps or you could ask someone from your church. Or..."

Sandra sighed. "I suppose I should try one of the dating apps, though I really don't want to. I don't have much time."

"I know." Mya's face lit. "Maybe go hang out in the produce department at one of those fancy grocery stores." Her eyes widened. "Let's go together. I'll be your wing woman, and you can be mine."

Sandra nodded. It wasn't the worst idea, and it might work. "Why not? Want to go now?"

Mya made a face. "Dressed like that?" She waved a hand toward Sandra.

Sandra looked down at her cleaning clothes. "Hmm. Good point. I don't want to go home to shower and change though. My grandmother would want to know why. Plus, I kind of snuck out of the house."

"No way." Mya shook her head. "This is worse than I realized. You not being open and honest with your grandma is a big deal. Is there more going on here?"

Sandra drew in a breath and let it out in a puff between her lips like air escaping from a balloon. "I can't do anything right. No matter what it is, it's not good enough. She's always been picky, but lately she's taken it to the next level."

"I'm sorry. I remember you mentioning things had gotten rough, but I didn't realize it was bothering you so much. Is there something else going on? You usually manage your grandma's demands better."

Sandra started to shake her head but stopped. "Well, things at the diner are kind of crazy right now. Our chef quit, and Adela is back. My aunt thinks the sun rises and sets with her. In a way, I get it. Adela is beautiful, successful, has an amazing daughter, can cook like..." Her mouth watered thinking about Adela's recent creations. "Let's just say the woman has a gift. But she's not going to stick around. She'll be off to her next big adventure before you know it. I'm here. I'm not going anywhere, but my aunt doesn't see me as an equal. It's so frustrating. I'm expected to keep things going on a shoestring budget, and it's not working. I want Romero's to succeed long term, not just when Adela decides to grace us with her presence."

Mya furrowed her brows. "No wonder your grandma is getting to you. I'm sorry." Her face brightened again. "I have an idea. Come back to my place. You can shower and wear something of mine. Then we can go find dates."

Sandra hesitated. She loved Mya, but her friend's taste in clothes was either short skirts or tight jeans, neither of which were Sandra's style. "I don't know. Do you think your clothes will fit me?"

"I'm sure I have something. You know I own practically every size."

Mya was a yo-yo dieter and probably did have something in her size. The biggest question now was would she feel comfortable wearing whatever fit from Mya's closet?

"Come on. You know you want to show your grandma you can find your own dates."

Sandra popped off the bench. "Fine. Let's go. I'll meet you at your apartment." Thirty minutes later, having showered, she wore Mya's robe and sat on her friend's bed as Mya dug through her closet. "Do you have any sundresses?"

Mya laughed. "Girl, you know me. I wouldn't be caught dead in a dress. Skirts are it for me."

This was such a bad idea. Sandra would never attract the kind of man she wanted dressed like Mya.

Mya whirled around and held up a white mini skirt and a sleeveless red top. "What do you think? It's perfect for you. The skirt only skims the body and the top is modest."

She wrinkled her nose and stood. "I'll give it a try." She slipped into the outfit then stood in front of the mirror. The skirt came to her knees. "It's not a mini." She turned to the side. It looked good.

"You're a couple inches shorter than me, so it's longer on you."

"I like it, and it will look good with my sneakers too."

Mya rolled her eyes. "No way. You need sandals."

Sandra shook her head and pointed to her friend's feet. "I don't think so. You're an eight. I wear sevens."

"So what? It's only one size."

"I'll stick with my sneakers."

"But—"

Sandra raised her hand in the stop motion. "No. If a man isn't interested in me because I'm wearing sneakers, then he's not for me."

Mya rested a hand at her waist. "I thought you weren't actually looking for one. I thought the point was to fill a seat so to speak."

"True, but it'd be nice to have the possibility of a new friend."

"Okay. Whatever. Let's go." Mya had changed into a denim mini skirt and a white top with super cute sandals.

SANDRA REACHED FOR a plump orange, keeping an eye on the clientele of the closest nice grocery store to Mya's apartment. So far, she'd only spotted women or dads with their kids in tow. Where were all the single men?

Mya stood near the lemons. She cleared her throat and motioned with her head.

Sandra looked in that direction and gasped. Victor shopped here? Was that why his food tasted so good?

Victor's gaze met hers, and he smiled all the way to

his eyes. He strode toward her. "How's it going? Have you recovered from your dating disaster?"

She grimaced. "I'll survive. How was business today?"

"Great. Which is why I'm here. I need to restock."

She nodded. Too bad she couldn't ask Victor out. Her eyes widened. Why couldn't she? No. There was no point. Dating her competition, even if it was only for a single date, was a recipe for trouble. But if she was up front with him... "Victor?" Her voice squeaked. She cleared her throat. "I um...The thing is..."

He chuckled. "Just spit it out."

"I made a bet of sorts with my grandmother that she would never set me up on a blind date again if I could find one date a week for the next month."

He sobered. "That sounds serious."

"It is. I have to win this bet to save my sanity. I was wondering if maybe you'd be willing to go out with me this week as friends. No strings or expectations."

His eyes widened. "You want to go out with *me*?"

She chuckled. "Yes. I already know you, sort of, and you seem like a nice guy. What do you say? It's my treat, but we can't go anyplace too expensive, or it'll have to be Dutch."

Mirth shined in his eyes. "It would be my pleasure to treat you. In fact, I know the perfect place."

"Please don't say your food truck."

He crossed his arms. "Why not? You could be my guinea pig and try out a new dish I want to add to the menu."

FINDING LOVE IN SAN ANTONIO

"Absolutely not. I don't want you to work on our date."

His stance relaxed. "When you put it like that..."

They exchanged numbers and set the date and time.

Sandra pocketed her phone. "I'll text you when I figure out where we'll meet."

"Shouldn't I pick you up so your grandmother sees me? I mean you wouldn't want her to think you cheated."

She liked how this man thought. "You're right. If she has proof about my dates, then she can't try to wiggle out of our deal. I'll text our address too." Her breath caught when their gazes met. She could not fall for Victor no matter how much she was attracted to him and his gorgeous dark chocolate-colored eyes. She dragged her gaze away from him and toward Mya. "My friend is waiting for me. I should go. See you soon." She glanced back at him without looking above his nose. Then she fled toward her friend.

Mya's smile covered her face. She looked like she was ready to jump up and down in celebration.

"Don't you dare." Sandra slipped her arm through Mya's and pulled her out of the produce department.

"He's so cute!"

Sandra put a finger to her lips. "Shh. He'll hear you." She glanced over her shoulder. No sign of Victor. She breathed a little easier.

"Sorry. I take it you accomplished your mission?" Mya asked.

"Yes. We can go back so you can meet someone after Victor leaves."

"I can't believe you asked a stranger out on a date."

Sandra guided her friend to the other side of the grocery store. "He's technically not a stranger. He owns the food truck that parks around the corner from Romero's."

"Interesting."

"What's that supposed to mean."

Mya shrugged. "Nothing. But we don't have to find me a date. Since you know this guy, I'm not worried about you."

Sandra slowed and tilted her head. She had much to be grateful for, and Mya was on that list. "You sure you don't want to stick around? I don't mind."

"Honestly, it sounded exciting at first, but the more I thought about it, the more I wasn't looking forward to asking out a stranger."

"Everyone starts out as a stranger." Sandra didn't want to push her friend if she really didn't want to do this, but she also wanted to give her a little nudge in case she was backing out due to fear.

"True, but I'm good with leaving date-free."

"Okay." Sandra altered course for the exit. Victor stood in line. He shopped fast. She ducked her chin and rushed out hoping he wouldn't notice she hadn't bought anything. Butterflies filled her stomach. She had a date with Victor! She needed to get it together. There was no way they could be more than friends. Absolutely no way.

THE DOORBELL RANG. Sandra glanced in the mirror at the

entryway and then opened the door. Her breath caught. Victor cleaned up well. The black short-sleeved button up and chino pants complemented his brown skin tone and eyes. She smiled. "You look nice."

"So do you." He grinned and poked his head inside. "Should I meet your grandmother?" he asked softly.

"Yes." She stepped aside, allowing him to enter. She'd chosen to wear a midi dress and strappy sandals and left her hair down to give her head a break from the ponytail she'd worn to work earlier. It appeared the extra time she'd spent primping had paid off. Not that she had been trying to impress him. She simply liked to look her best.

She led the way to the living room where Abuela sat in her chair reading. "Grandma, this is Victor. We are going out to dinner."

Abuela stood and turned. Her eyes widened and then narrowed. "I expect you to treat my granddaughter with respect."

"Yes, ma'am. Sandra is a special lady. I would never be unkind or disrespectful to her—at least not on purpose."

Abuela nodded. "*Bueno.* Have a nice dinner." She turned, sat, and then resumed reading.

Interesting. What had Abuela been thinking? Clearly, she'd been surprised by Victor, but Sandra had told Abuela she had a date so that part wasn't new. She shook off the thought as she strolled beside Victor to his modest SUV.

Victor opened the passenger door for her.

"You don't have to be so nice," she said.

He raised a brow. "Good manners are not being nice." He closed the door and a moment later, slid into the driver's seat. "I hope you don't mind, but I made us a reservation at Bourbon Street Seafood Kitchen on the Riverwalk."

"Nice." She only hoped she could afford it. He'd offered to treat, but she had no intention of letting him. "I love seafood."

"Whew. I took a risk making that reservation. I'm glad you're not upset."

She'd had something more modest in mind, but the idea of a nice restaurant on the Riverwalk sounded incredibly romantic. "There's no way my grandmother will think this isn't a real date after I tell her where we went." She'd try and remember to take some pictures too.

Victor glanced her way then focused forward as he navigated traffic. "It is a real date. I didn't forget the no strings attached and that it's a date between friends."

Sandra blew out a breath of relief. For a second, she'd been afraid he'd read more into the invite than she'd intended. She had to admit, so far, this night ranked far above the blind dates her grandmother had set up for her. "How is it you're single? You seem like a great guy."

"Thanks. I've been focused on my business. It's all-consuming."

"About that. You must be exhausted working seven days a week."

"It's not so bad. I cater to the lunch crowd. Now and then, I'll stay open through dinner, but it's not something I do often."

How had she not realized that? "I guess that would make it easier. It also leaves room for outside activities." She slid a glance in his direction to see if he caught her suggestion that he had plenty of time to date.

"Yes. I coach boys' basketball too."

"Yikes. Now I understand why you're so busy. Doesn't basketball have a long season?" She always imagined anyone who played basketball would be super tall. Victor didn't look much over five foot ten, but if he was good with kids and knew the game, coaching made sense. He was definitely a people person.

"The pros do, but this is a community team, and the season is pretty short by comparison. In fact, it's about to wrap up." Victor tightened his hands on the steering wheel as they came into some especially heavy traffic downtown.

"Cool."

"Yeah. It's fun and the kids are great...at least most of them are." He signaled and pulled into a parking lot. "It's busy here tonight. I hope we can find a parking spot."

She scanned the rows of cars and waved toward the next row over. "There's one over there."

The SUV surged forward and headed in that direction. "Thanks. I forgot how difficult parking can be here."

"It's not someplace I frequent for that very reason. This is a huge treat." She didn't like traffic either. "I'm glad you drove, and we didn't meet here. I seriously dislike driving in this area."

Victor pulled into the parking spot she'd pointed out

and killed the engine. "I'm happy to drive. Stay put, and I'll get your door."

She almost told him he didn't need to but remembered he considered it good manners. Her door swung open. She stepped out. The energy of the Riverwalk surged around her even from the parking lot. A thrill of excitement shot through her. She almost never came here, but it was such a fun place to visit. She breathed in the food-scented air, and her stomach rumbled. "This is the most fun I've had on a date since forever."

"Lady, you need to step up your dating game." He guided them to the Riverwalk entrance.

She chuckled. "Agreed. Guess that's why I'm with you."

"You know it." He grinned and winked playfully.

She strolled beside him along the river, taking in the foliage and gentle flow of the river. In spite of all the people, serenity enveloped her. They walked across a footbridge. She slowed to admire flowers along the bank. A short while later they strolled into the restaurant and were immediately seated at an outside table. To her way of thinking, the evening couldn't get more romantic. She sucked in a breath. This was a date between friends, nothing more. Neither of them had time for romantic entanglements.

"Everything okay?" Victor looked at her with concern in his eyes.

"Yep." She looked over the menu. "Everything looks delicious." Though a little pricey for her wallet, she would be able to manage it if she didn't make a habit of going to places like this. It was definitely worth the price simply for the experience.

"I agree. But I know what I'm getting." Victor placed his menu on the table. "Do you know what you want?"

"I think I'm going to get the naked fish with white rice."

His eyes widened. "Good choice. You sure you don't want anything fancier?"

"I am. Simple is nice. What about you?"

"I planned to order the same."

She chuckled. "Are *you* sure you don't want anything fancier?" she teased.

"Positive."

Sandra placed her menu on top of his.

A moment later their waiter took their order and then moved on to another table.

"Tell me about yourself. I know where you go to church and where you work, as well as a bit about your family dynamics, but tell me about you."

"There's not all that much to tell. I have a business management degree I hope to put to good use at Romero's. I'd like to take over running the place when my aunt is ready to retire."

"Good for you. What else?"

Her mind blanked. Wasn't that enough? Victor was a far cry from Anthony who'd demeaned her when she told him her plan. "I don't know what more to say."

"Hobbies?"

"None. Unless you count meeting my best friend Mya at the coffee shop once a week."

He tilted his head to the side. "I don't believe you. I know there's more to you than work. I'm guessing you like fashion magazines."

She sucked in a breath. "I do. But I'm not obsessed. How did you know that?"

He dipped his chin. "I saw one on the floor of your pickup when I stopped to check on you."

She chuckled. "You can add sleuth to the list of things one should know about Victor."

"Not really." He reached for his ice water. "Just observant."

They bantered back and forth for at least twenty minutes about the restaurant business. She could talk shop all day. "Do you plan to expand to a second truck in the future?"

"I'm considering it, but it's a lot of work, and there's only one of me."

She nodded.

Their waiter arrived and placed meals in front of each of them. "Is there anything else I can get you?"

"I'm good." Sandra breathed in the heavenly scent. She loved the smell of cooked salmon.

"Same. Thanks." Victor glanced at her with a twinkle in his eyes. "Want me to bless the food?"

"Sure." Now that was a first for any of her dates. Abuela would be impressed. Sandra closed her eyes and bowed her head.

"Lord, we thank You for this delicious-smelling meal and ask that You would bless it to our bodies. Amen."

"Amen." She reached for her fork. "I don't mean to

gush, but this was a really good idea."

He sat a little taller. "I'm glad."

Comfortable silence settled between them as they ate.

She really liked Victor, but he had to stay in the friend zone no matter what.

"I was thinking," Victor said. "You mentioned needing to find a date for four weeks in a row. How about if we hang out again like this next week so you won't have to wait in the supermarket for an unsuspecting man to show up to ask out?"

She nearly choked on her food but quickly washed it down with water. "You knew?"

He chuckled. "It was pretty obvious. Especially when you walked out with your friend empty-handed."

Her face heated. "I'm so embarrassed."

"Don't be. I count myself blessed to have been at the right place at the right time. What do you say? Want to hang out again next week? My team has a game, but we could get dessert after."

"You're inviting me to watch your team play?" Definitely a friend-zone kind of date.

He nodded. "Do you mind?"

"No. Not at all. It sounds like fun. Text me the details, and I'll meet you there." Clearly, she'd read too much into this evening. Disappointment and relief mingled in her. She finished off her water and then reached for her purse. "You ready to go?" She already paid their bill, so they were free to leave anytime.

He stood. "That was good. Thanks for treating. I'll

cover dessert next week."

"You bet you will." She grinned. He'd tried to pay, but she'd slipped her credit card to the waiter first.

They strolled side-by-side, retracing their steps from earlier. She couldn't wait to tell Abuela about tonight. There was no way her grandmother would be setting her up on blind dates ever again. One problem down, two to go. Somehow, she had to convince Tía Soccoro Romero's was in good hands with her, but to do that, she needed to deliver, and she also needed to figure out what had Abuela so uptight of late.

# Chapter Twelve

THE FOLLOWING DAY, ADELA PUT HER heart into cooking the most delicious meal she could make out of the fresh produce and other supplies they'd purchased at the market. Soccoro and Fabi sat in the kitchen of Romero's at a small table, watching and waiting while she sprinkled chopped cilantro and parsley. She slid a plate of chalupas in front of the two, sat opposite them, her elbows propped on the table and chin resting in her cupped hands, and waited.

Soccoro took a bite, and then another, chewing slowly and experimentally. Finally, she looked up at Adela. "Stop looking at me like that. All right. I'll admit it. It's better than what we were serving before. But I can't afford to buy everything we need at those prices."

Fabi took another bite and grinned. "This is fantastic, Mom. Really good! I didn't think I was very hungry, but I might want another one when I finish this."

Adela arched her brows at her mother-in-law. "See? Out of the mouths of babes."

Fabi shot her a dirty look. "I am not a baby, Mom. Good grief."

Adela waved her hand. "It's just a saying. I know you're all grown up now at the ancient age of thirteen."

She turned her attention back to Soccoro. "Seriously. Food like this could turn your business around once word gets out. Can't you move a few things in the budget to make room for better ingredients?"

"No." Soccoro dabbed at her lips with a napkin. "There is no room to move anything. I have almost strangled the budget to keep this place open." She took a deep breath. "I've been thinking of selling Romero's."

"What?" Shock hit Adela so hard it rocked her.

"No, way, Abuela! You can't sell Romero's. It's part of our family." Fabi thumped her glass of soda on the table so hard it splashed over the edge.

Soccoro pushed away from the table and walked over to a wall lined with photos, many of them old and starting to fade. Adela had that wall memorized...the same picture of her and Mauricio that was in his old bedroom graced that wall along with ones of Soccoro and her husband who'd died years ago. "This was our dream. To open a restaurant in America, to have a legacy for our family. But I'm too old to breathe new life into this place. And there are investors willing to pay a nice price for the property."

Adela pushed away from the table and walked over to Soccoro. She placed her arm around the older woman's shoulders and gave her a hug. "Romero's is more than a piece of property. It's home. It has meaning to all of us. Mauricio and I met and fell in love here. Fabi grew up playing in this kitchen when she was small."

Fabi came over and leaned her head against Soccoro's other side. "You can't sell it, Abuela. We all love it too much. We'll help you keep it, won't we, Mom?"

Adela nodded. "Yes. I can do more than just help in the kitchen. How about if we revamp the menu? Put new dishes on it that will draw in more customers? Maybe raise the prices just a little since many of your menu items have stayed the same for thirty years. I know you've changed a few, but not much. Maybe it's time?"

Soccoro shrugged. She wrapped an arm around Adela and Fabi and squeezed and then stepped away. "I don't know. I'm not sure I have the heart for it anymore."

"Don't give up yet. Let's wait a bit to think and pray, okay?" Adela looked at Soccoro and Fabi, but her daughter didn't meet her eyes. Was she feeling the same sense of defeat Soccoro seemed to be dealing with? She couldn't let that happen—she loved them too much to let their spirits be crushed. "Soccoro?"

Her mother-in-law hunched a shoulder. "Maybe. I don't know. I guess it won't make things any worse than they are now."

Adela reached out and gripped Soccoro's hand. "That's the spirit. We won't give up. I'm going to get to work right now and whip up a few new dishes for customers to try. You'll see. We can make this a success. I know we can."

An hour later, Sandra came up to the serving window, her order pad in her hand. She ripped off the top page and slid it under the hook on the swiveling holder and then spun it toward Adela. "*Uno burrito de frijoles.* Customers are coming in, and things are going to get busy soon."

Adela placed a plate on the window and shoved it toward Sandra. "Try this, *por favor?*"

Sandra stared at the plate containing a steaming hot lamb tamale and a fork and then looked back to Adela. "What is this? It doesn't look like a burrito to me."

"Just try it, please?" Adela waved at the tamale.

"Why? I need the burrito. I don't have time to eat."

"Humor me, okay? I want to know what you think." Adela crossed her arms and took a step away from the window, hoping her cousin-in-law would pick up the fork and try her newest creation. Maybe she could help convince Soccoro to add something more exotic like this to the menu.

Soccoro moved closer and picked up the fork and then handed it to Sandra. "Try a bite. I'd like to know what you think. Gracias."

Sandra cut through the tamale with the fork, placed a bite in her mouth, and chewed.

"Well?" Soccoro and Adela chimed at the same time.

"It's good. What is it, lamb?"

Adela beamed and shot a look at Fabi and then at Soccoro. "See? I told you it's good."

Sandra hunched a shoulder. "Yeah. It's good. But lamb won't work at Romero's. It's too highbrow. And it's too expensive. I still need that burrito."

Fabi gave a sad shake of her head. "Told you so, Mom. We can't serve lamb. It's too much."

"Yeah, yeah. I'll get that burrito now."

"Don't be disappointed, mija." Soccoro gave Adela a gentle smile. "You know Romero's has always catered to working-class people. We need to stick with the foods they like and will accept, as well as what they can afford."

Adela whirled around. "Fine. But at least try to meet me halfway?"

"Lamb is not halfway, mija."

Sandra held out her hand for the plated burrito. "Right. Like I said, it's expensive."

Adela huffed. "Thanks for the feedback." Her phone buzzed in her pocket, and she slipped it out. Who would be contacting her when she was in the middle of cooking? Maybe David? No. Of course not. He didn't have her phone number, and there'd be no reason for him to text. If he wanted another interview, God forbid, he'd touch base with her agent.

She glanced at the phone and cringed. Matias. Right when she was thinking of her agent, he had to text and remind her he was still waiting for an answer about the European tour. And she didn't have one to give him.

AN HOUR LATER, Adela sank into a chair at a small table only a few feet from the pick-up window in Romero's. The lunch crowd was past, and she'd asked Sandra and Soccoro to take over for a few minutes while she got off her feet and took a break. The intensity of the lunch rush was great for income, but not so great for her feet.

The bell on the door jingled and a man who appeared to be in his early sixties strolled in. He glanced around and then headed for the pick-up window, his pleasant features warming into a smile as his gaze landed on Soccoro. Salt and pepper hair cut neatly on the sides and short on top gave him a distinguished air as did the cut of his casual clothing and his purposeful stride as he neared the window.

He lifted a hand as he neared. "Ladies, how is your day going? I called in an order, Sandra."

She slid a bag across the counter. "Here you go, Patrick. Still hot. It just came off the grill."

Soccoro swiveled, and her face brightened in a smile. "Patrick. How is my favorite business owner? Staying busy at the gym?" She gave him a long look. "It appears you've been spending a bit of time pumping iron and not sitting behind the desk answering calls or helping clients. You look very fit." She walked over to the counter and leaned toward him.

Adela's eyes widened. Interesting. Was she sensing a hint of interest in her mother-in-law toward this nice-looking man? She set down her coffee cup and leaned back, wondering where this conversation might be headed.

Patrick grinned in return. "Thanks. My son finished his term in the Marines, and he's returned home to stay. I've spent the last few weeks demonstrating all the routines on our machines and training him to run the business. My goal is to retire soon and only be there for backup when he needs extra help."

Soccoro straightened, her brows rising and her mouth forming a small O. "Really? You're retiring? I had no idea you were thinking of doing that."

"Yes, I've actually been considering it for some time

now. With Patrick, Jr., home for good, it feels right. Know what I mean? Like it's time to give something else a chance. Maybe spread my wings a bit. Travel, maybe? Or sit in my easy chair for a bit and figure out what my next step is."

Soccoro drew in a deep breath and let it out on a sigh. "Retirement. I can't even imagine what that would be like. Rest and relaxation, that's what I'd go for. I can travel through my TV set."

Patrick laughed. "Do you ever think about hanging up your apron once and for all?"

"Ha! Only every day. But I can't see that happening anytime soon. I will probably keep going as long as we can keep the doors open and the lights on. I pray about it often."

"I'll pray about it for you as well, and I'll do my share to help make that happen. Romero's is my favorite place to eat when I have time to get away from the gym. Once I retire, you'll see a lot more of me."

Soccoro's worried expression softened. "Thank you, Patrick. I'd like that."

He gave a small wave and headed to the door, and then half-turned, looked over his shoulder and hesitated. Then he spun back around and went out the door.

Adela picked up her mug and took a sip of the warm coffee—now what was all that about? She'd never seen Soccoro show interest in any man before, but there had definitely been something. Only time would tell if it was more than friendship or not. "Soccoro?" She waited until her mother-in-law turned and glanced at her. "I need to return a call. I'm going to step out where it's quiet. I shouldn't be long."

"Sí. Whatever you need. Take your time, mija."

Adela had put off the call to her agent longer than she should have. It was time to deal with this, one way or the other. She slipped out the back door into the relative quiet and breathed in the summer-scented air, loving the fragrance of the nearby river and the abundant flowers and trees blooming at intervals along the walk. She hit speed dial and waited for Matias to answer. "Matias? It's Adela. I'm sorry for taking so long to get back to you."

"Adela. You were supposed to call me with an answer yesterday." Clear frustration edged his voice with the first words out of his mouth. "The network is breathing down my neck. They have sponsors waiting for an answer. You know how this works."

Adela blew out a soft exhale. She did know, all too well. "I'm sorry, Matias. Fabi doesn't want to leave San Antonio. I promised her we'd be here for the summer, and I can't pull her away a week after we arrived. She blew up when I tried to talk to her about it."

"But you can't pass up this amazing opportunity, Adela. It's career changing. It could set you up for the rest of your life."

Adela sank down onto an iron bench under a tree. "Which is why I need more time. I can't push Fabi. It's not fair."

Silence greeted her for several seconds. "Well..." Matias appeared to be weighing their options. "Maybe playing a little hard to get will work in our favor when we negotiate terms."

"If we negotiate, Matias. I'm not making any promises. I've decided it must be Fabi's decision. I would never forgive myself if I alienated my daughter for the sake of my career. It's not worth that."

"She'll love Europe, Adela. I guarantee it. You just need to put a little pressure on her, that's all. Tell her about all the cute boys over there. She'd look marvelous riding behind a guy on a Vespa."

Adela jerked upright. "She is not riding a Vespa. And certainly not with some teenage boy I don't know, or any boy for that matter! Are you out of your mind, Matias?"

Adela heard footsteps behind her, and she turned her head. Fabi. How much had she heard?

"Mom? Abuela wants you to come in. She said you have a visitor."

DAVID LEANED AGAINST the counter in Romero's as the amazing aromas wafted around him, making his stomach growl. He'd eaten a rushed lunch that felt long ago and too small. Maybe he'd grab something more while he waited for Adela. He'd been disappointed when he walked in and spotted Soccoro and Fabi but he hadn't seen Adela. He turned to Soccoro. "Is she out running an errand? I can come back later if it's more convenient."

"No. She just took a break from work. She's out back resting and making a phone call."

"A break? Where does she work? I thought she was in San Antonio on vacation from filming. Did they set up a studio here in town somewhere?"

Soccoro chuckled. "She's working for me. At least for a few days. My cook quit, and Adela stepped in."

Adela strode through the swinging doors that led from the kitchen to the colorful dining area. David stood as she approached. His heart sank when he didn't see a glimmer of a smile or sign of welcome in her eyes. Had he annoyed her somehow? Maybe a light, teasing touch would bring her around. "Hey, working here as a cook, huh? I thought you Hollywood-types only cooked in front of a camera, not for real people." As soon as the words were out of his mouth, he regretted them.

The corners of her lips turned even further down, if that were possible. "What are you doing here?" She planted her hands on her hips.

"Wow." He held up his palms. "Sorry. No need to snap. I was only teasing."

"Mija." Soccoro hurried forward and tapped Adela on the shoulder. "What is wrong with you? Why didn't you say something? David is practically family. There's no need to be rude to him."

She spun around, her mouth agape. Then she snapped it shut. "Family? I have no idea what you mean." She waved from Soccoro to David. "You two know each other?"

"Of course. He used to work here years ago. Not full time or anything, more of a summer job. Surely, you remember? You worked here at the same time."

David tried to muster a grin, but in the face of Adela's suspicious expression, it didn't quite make it. "Just for one summer, and it was years ago, so you probably don't remember. I was a line cook back then."

Adela's eyes widened. "Davey? It's coming back to me. You've changed so much. Your hair was much longer and wavy. And your face was—"

"I know." He stopped her before she said something embarrassing. He still cringed thinking about his baby face years ago and skin issues. "Thankfully, I outgrew both of those things."

She crossed her arms over her chest. "You were also kind, sweet, and thoughtful. It appears you grew out of those things as well."

"Thanks for that vote of confidence." David almost laughed this time, trying to keep the edge of sarcasm out of his voice. That wouldn't do anything to help the situation with Adela.

Soccoro stood to the side, watching with brows raised.

"So, Davey, what did you want besides something to eat. Fabi said I had a visitor. You wanted to talk to me for some reason?"

"Yes, I did. I was wondering if I could profile you for *The Telegram*? The interview got a ton of play online, and when I mentioned bumping into you, my editor was interested in a follow-up piece."

"No way! Tell your editor my answer is a big fat no. I'm not going through that again."

"Adela!" Soccoro took a step and stopped in front of Adela. "Don't be rude to our customers or to someone we've known for years who is part of our Romero family. This is not like you, mija."

"Did you watch the last interview, Soccoro? He trashed me and *Alta Cocina*. I worked for years to achieve my own television show, and I'm not going to let him humiliate me again, even if he did carry my groceries to my car and treat me decently the last time I saw him." She threw David a narrowed-eyed look, but she uncrossed her arms.

She remembered that, did she? Maybe he'd scored at least one small point with their talk at the market. "But it would be your chance to explain anything you wanted to. In your own words...to anyone who tunes in. Think of the opportunity. You might even mention working at Romero's now if you want to."

The young girl he'd met on the soccer field and seen again at the market popped through the swinging kitchen doors. "She'll do it. Yes!" She gave a fist pump and grinned.

"Fabi!" Adela pivoted toward her.

"And who is this?" David couldn't resist a smile at the young teen with the glowing face.

"She's my daughter. Fabiola, but we call her Fabi." Adela's stance softened, and her mouth twitched as though she were trying not to smile.

"Do it, Mom. It's free publicity for Romero's. He's going to let you talk about it too, so what do you have to lose?"

David chuckled. "She has me there. I did say that, and I don't break my word. You might want to listen to your daughter. I like her."

Adela frowned, but it didn't reach her eyes. "You

stay out of this." She turned to Fabi again. "When did you get so smart to think of publicity?"

This time David laughed out loud.

Adela sighed. "Fine. I give up. I'm outnumbered. When and where?"

"Tomorrow at three o'clock on the Riverwalk near the bridge closest to your restaurant. Does that work for your schedule? It's after lunch but before dinner."

Adela nodded. "It's a date." She covered her lips with her fingers. "I mean...I'll meet you there. But you'd better be a lot nicer this time than the last time."

He gave her a slightly wicked grin. "I know how to be nice, *Miss Adela*. I'll come with my best manners tomorrow, I promise. I look forward to seeing you there again."

# Chapter Thirteen

ADELA FIDDLED WITH THE STRAP OF her purse, suddenly nervous at meeting David again outside of the somewhat safe confines of the restaurant and her family surrounding her. It seemed beyond silly that she, a world-wise TV star, should experience nerves from an interview with a newsman, but...this wasn't just any newsman. She rubbed her hands on the chilled flesh of her upper arms. It was hot today...and humid. Having chills thinking about David? What had gotten into her lately? Someone touched her shoulder, and she jumped.

"Sorry." David chuckled and stepped around to her side where she could see him. "Didn't mean to startle you. What had you so immersed in thought that you didn't hear me come up behind you?"

Heat rose to her cheeks and chased away the chill. No way would she tell him she'd been thinking about him. "Oh, lost in the beauty of my surroundings, I guess." She waved at the canal in front of them with the colorful boats filled with tourists that drifted past. It wasn't a lie— she loved sitting here and had been very aware of the shade cast by the trees, the sounds of birds calling and chirping, and the soothing fragrance and sound of the water.

He nodded and tipped his head toward the foot bridge over the canal leading from the rows of shops where they stood to the other side of the canal. "Want to go stand on the bridge and chat there?"

She arched a brow. "Chat? Or start the interview?"

"I guess a bit of both." He held up his small recorder. "I'll turn it on now if you don't mind." He clicked it on before she had a chance to reply.

She stepped out before he could start moving and walked to the center of the bridge, hoping to regain her composure before she had to start answering questions. What would he ask her? Would it be as awful as that first interview before she returned to San Antonio?

David stopped beside her and leaned on the railing looking down into the slow-moving water and then turned and shot her a devastating grin. "Were you born in San Antonio?"

She almost pressed her hand over her heart to try to stop the insane fluttering, but she caught herself in time. Instead, she frowned. "You know the answer to that, so why are you asking?"

"Humor me, okay?"

"San Antonio, born and raised." She glanced out at a passing boat carrying a couple about her age—he had his arm around her shoulders, and her head rested against him—the picture of love and contentment. Would she ever know anything close to that again?

"How did you get into cooking?" David nudged her with his elbow. "Adela. You're lost again."

She waved a hand toward the boat drifting on down

the canal. "Sorry. It's so peaceful here, even with all the people." She drew in a deep breath of the fragrance surrounding her and then let it out slowly. "My mother taught me when I was young. When Dad cooked at our house, I always wanted to help. But my idea of helping at that young age was grabbing the salt or sugar and giving his food a helping dose." She smiled at the memory. "So Mom taught me to cook properly to save Dad's creations from being ruined. When I was a little older, I assisted him in the kitchen."

"That was the extent of your training?" David positioned the recorder a little closer to Adela.

"No. My dad died from cancer my last year of high school. Raul Romero, Soccoro's husband and the original owner of Romero's, hired me as a line cook the summer of my senior year. That was my culinary school and so much more."

"What do you mean so much more?"

"Everything good in my life has come from Romero's. I worked there almost ten years. It's where I met and fell in love with my husband, Mauricio. Raul and Soccoro became my family. When Raul passed, Soccoro and Mauricio managed the place, and I became head cook. It was because of our success that I started doing segments for *San Antonio in the Morning* and then on my local show and *Alta Cocina*."

"Speaking of *Alta Cocina*, you film that in L.A. What brought you back to San Antonio this summer, and what's going on with Romero's? Are you pitching in while you're home short-term, or is there anything in the works that will keep you here longer?"

"I came back to spend time with family—my daughter needed time with her grandmother, and I agreed—it was time to leave L.A. and return to our hometown for a while." She almost blurted out she had a European offer in the works, but she bit her tongue. No need to let the tabloids get hold of that tidbit, especially since she hadn't made a decision yet. "I'm working on a new menu. The old favorites, but with some new twists. Not to mention, better ingredients. All locally-sourced— if I can get Soccoro on board."

David shifted his position and nodded toward a bench. "Want to sit down for a bit while we finish this?" He gave a wicked grin. "Or should we hop on one of the tour boats and pretend we're a couple like the one you were watching when we first got here?"

Warmth rose to Adela's cheeks again. He was definitely too observant. She followed him to the wrought iron and wood bench and settled beside him, but not too close. She didn't think her heart could take that. "Is that all you have to ask me?"

He laughed. "Almost. Soccoro is one tough cookie when it comes to her restaurant, that's for sure."

Adela relaxed and smiled. "The toughest."

"How about a sneak peak of any of the new dishes?"

"Not just yet. I'm still kind of in the experimentation phase." She placed her hand over her heart. "But please don't write that!"

"How about something like 'she was coy with her response'?"

This time Adela laughed out loud. David was so

much more relaxed—and kinder—than he'd been in that first interview. "Coy. That's good. A lot better than 'she has no clue.'"

"Can you talk about the food a little bit? I'm sure you've kicked around a few ideas."

"I want to show San Antonio what I've learned in L.A. the past five years and keep the low price point. Romero's has been around three decades, but I want to make the city see us with new eyes. To fall in love all over again."

He arched a brow. "Fall in love? That's what you're hoping for while you're here in our fair city?"

Adela rolled her eyes. "No. I mean, I'm hoping the people in this town will fall in love with Romero's—with our food—all over again."

"Then you aren't interested in falling in love again personally? I'm sure your fans would love to know."

She turned her head away a few inches and bit her lip. "Let's keep the questions a little less personal, okay?"

He hesitated for only a split second then clicked off the recorder. "Right. Sorry about that. I did promise to be on my best behavior this time, didn't I?"

"You did."

He slid the device into his pocket. "Thank you for your time. I think that wraps up the interview for today. I really appreciate you meeting me here and doing this."

Adela let out a little sigh and smiled. "It was better than what I expected, based on the first one, so I'm glad you kept your word. But you should thank my daughter, not me."

"I will the next time I see her."

"When will you run the story?"

"It should come out in a few days—a week at most. Will you have the menu finished by then?"

"I suppose anything is possible."

He reached over and touched her hand lightly. "I have a good feeling. This article might bring a lot of patrons into Romero's who want to try out your new menu items."

Tingles ran up her arm from his touch, but she didn't move her hand. She almost slipped her fingers through his but realized what she'd been thinking and eased back. "A good feeling, huh? This from the man who said I was out of touch during the last interview?"

He had the grace to wince. "I'm sorry about that. It wasn't kind, and it wasn't true."

"What makes you such an expert on food, anyway? Did you work somewhere in the culinary industry besides Romero's?"

He laughed. "So you're interviewing me now?"

"Maybe, *Davey*." She giggled. "Turn about and all that, you know."

DAVID STOOD AND held out his hand. "Want to walk for a moment since we're just chatting now?"

Adela nodded and took his hand in hers as she rose to her feet.

David was very aware of the woman beside him, and he didn't release his grip but pulled her a little closer to

MIRALEE FERRELL and KIMBERLY ROSE JOHNSON

his side. What a relief that she didn't tug her hand away. "Romero's was my first and only experience in the restaurant business. Watching you command the kitchen made me realize I didn't have it in me to be a chef. I'm better at eating food than cooking it."

"When did you start writing for *The Telegram*? Didn't you go to college on the east coast?"

"Good memory. Yeah, NYU. I wrote for food and wine magazines after school. Then one fall, I came home to visit my parents and found myself inspired by the food scene here. And decided to move back."

"San Antonio was more inspiring than New York? Are you serious?"

"Definitely. And as long as I'm being honest, I have a confession to make." He hesitated and looked into her eyes as a hint of pink rose in his cheeks. "I was a big fan of your first show, *Adela's Kitchen*. I saw every episode."

"Really? Tell me more."

The look of astonishment and joy on Adela's face made David as warm inside as her cheeks had been a moment ago. "The food you made was simple and tasty with a lot of local influence. It was always something that I could make at home without totally messing up. Also..."

"Also...?"

"Also, I had a big crush on you going back to the Romero's days. So, there's that."

He gazed more deeply into her eyes, wishing for a brief heartbeat that he dared lean down and kiss her, but her shocked expression made him take a step away. That may not have been the best thing to share.

"Oh! Well... That's um... That's..."

"Sorry, I shouldn't have said that."

"No. You're fine." She tore her eyes away from him and swiveled the other direction, bumping into a tall man carrying two ice cream cones.

The man struggled to balance the cones and righted them before they tipped onto the street. "I'm so sorry, miss."

"No, it was totally my fault. I wasn't looking where I was going. I'm sorry." She brushed at her lapel to rub off the ice cream.

"Not a problem." He tipped his head and walked away.

"Allow me." David took the napkin. "You have a little ice cream on your nose as well." He carefully wiped away the ice cream, his heart beating faster at the nearness of her lips. Time to change the direction of his thoughts—and fast. "Now I'm in the mood for ice cream. How about you?"

Adela smiled. "Always." She grinned. "If this doesn't take care of your false ideas about me, I don't know what will."

"You're right. You're much more down to earth than I thought. You're a lot more like I remembered years ago when I worked at Romero's."

She smirked. "Down to earth. Is that good?"

"It is." That smirk of hers was a bit too enticing. He scrambled for neutral ground. "I have a reading this weekend. My first book is published. It's about the history of Tex-Mex cooking."

Adela raised her brows. "Davey's got a book out? Wow! I had no idea."

"I'm not the best public speaker. Actually, it sort of terrifies me. But afterward, there's a little party. Great food. I think you'd have fun if you'd care to come?"

"I'll have to see what's going on at Romero's... But, maybe."

That wasn't the answer he'd been hoping for—at least it wasn't a no. "Cool. Maybe, it is."

Adela bit her lip as though reconsidering or wondering if she'd hurt his feelings. "Um...I need to walk over to the soccer field and check on Fabi. It's only about five blocks from here, and I could use the exercise. Want to walk with me?" She pushed a strand of hair out of her eyes. "Of course, if you're busy, I understand, but I do need to go."

He grinned. "Not busy at all. I'd love to see Fabi play." *And walk with you another five blocks*, he inserted mentally and moved out to keep pace with her brisk stride.

FABIOLA HADN'T FELT this lonely in a long time. She loved being in San Antonio, but she hadn't really met anyone to play soccer with yet. Getting in a few drills on her own today had been a good idea, but she'd been kind of hoping the kids who were here last time might show up again. Thirty minutes or so later, she took a breather as something whacked her calf from the back. She spun around and plucked a soccer ball off the grass.

A kid about her age jogged toward her—a cute boy with a shy smile—she kind of thought he'd been here a few days ago when she'd been hanging out. "This yours?"

"Yeah." He waved a hand in the air when he was about ten yards out. "I'll grab it."

She grinned and kicked it toward him—right into his hands. "Nope. It's all good."

He slowed as he got within a few feet and then tucked the ball under his arm. "Nice kick."

"Thanks. But you know you're not supposed to catch it with your hands, right?"

"I'm the goalie, so it's cool. My name's Brandon. I think I've seen you here before, right? You on a local team?"

"I'm Fabi. My mom and I are visiting my grandmother for the summer. I was on a team in L.A. when we lived there, but I haven't found one in San Antonio."

"You can hang out with us anytime. We're usually here around this time every Monday, Wednesday, and Friday during the summer."

Fabi smiled. "Cool. Are you an official team?"

"Nah. Just having fun, which is why you can join us whenever. No pressure."

"Thanks. I might do that." Fabi waved as he turned to jog back to the mix of boys and girls in the distance. Very cool. It would be amazing to have kids her own age to play with again. She frowned as another thought hit her. As long as her mother didn't try to drag her off to Europe, right when she might be starting to fit into this

127

town again. Mom had promised not to make a decision without her, but Mom hadn't always kept her promises.

Brandon turned before he got to the kids, flashed her a smile, lifted his hand, and then pivoted and dashed the rest of the way to his friends.

Fabiola smiled as he moved into position at the goal at the far end of the field. Brandon. Yeah, it would be great to have a friend again, even if it was a boy.

"Fabi! Hey!" Fabi's heart sank. *Mom.* She'd forgotten her mother planned to stop by the field. She shielded her eyes from the glare of the sun. What was that news guy David doing with her? Strange. Mom walked closer but Fabi still raised her voice. "What do you want? You going to try and talk me into going to Europe again?"

Her mother slowed, glanced at David, then shook her head. "No. But I wish you'd be more open-minded."

Fabi crossed her arms over her chest. "Why do I have to be open-minded? Why don't you?"

ADELA FELT AS though she were fighting a losing battle that she had no hope of winning. Why were teens so hard to talk to? It didn't help that David was standing here taking in all the nuances of their family problems. "You remember David, don't you, Fabi?" She gestured toward him.

Fabi's expression brightened a little. "Yeah. Nice seeing you. You hanging out with my mom now?"

He stifled a chuckle. "We, uh, finished the interview, and I walked over with her...for the exercise, you know?

Hey, your mom says I have you to thank for getting that interview, so...thanks!"

"No problem. It was kind of a no-brainer." She rolled her eyes.

David grinned. "My office is a couple of blocks away, so I'll head on over there and let you ladies take care of business without me interfering."

Adela shot him a grateful look. "Thanks for the nice interview, Davey. Maybe I'll see you around." She waited until David had taken a few steps and then turned to her daughter. "I'm gonna go home and try out some more recipes for the menu, Fabi. Walk back with me?"

Fabi shrugged. "Whatever."

As Adela started across the grassy field, her phone buzzed. She pulled it out of her pocket and glanced at it— a text from Matias: Any updates? Adela frowned and then noticed the soccer ball rolling next to her.

Fabi leaned over, scooped it up, and then dribbled it beside her as she started walking across the grass toward the sidewalk.

Adela tucked her phone back into her pocket. Matias could wait until later. Right now, she needed this time with her daughter.

# Chapter Fourteen

ADELA KICKED OFF HER SHOES AFTER stepping through the front door of Soccoro's house and sighed. Why did every day seem to bring new problems? Although the interview had gone well, she wasn't too sure about attending Davey's reading. And she still needed to make a decision about Europe, or Matias would come unglued. She heard a sound in the kitchen—Soccoro's voice? She walked that direction and stopped in the doorway in time to see her mother-in-law petting her dog. "I thought you'd be at Romero's," Adela asked.

Fabiola stepped around her. "I'm gonna wash up."

"The dinner rush is over." Soccoro straightened and turned toward Adela. "I turned things over to Sandra and the prep cook for the night as I want the prep cook to have a little more responsibility. Besides, it was slow, and I figured the two of them could handle it this once. I want to hear all about the interview."

Adela pulled out a chair and sank in to it. "It was nice. You know David wrote for food and wine magazines in New York before *The Telegram*?"

"Yes? And?" She reached for the coffeepot. "How about a cup? Your usual with cream?

"That sounds lovely. Thank you. He invited me to a

book reading. He wrote a book. Did you know that?" She reached for the mug as Soccoro handed it across the table. "You're not having any?"

"I already did." She waved her hand. "*Qué onda, mija!* The interview sounds more like a date. Tell me more."

"Qué? No! I just—um—it wasn't like that."

Soccoro laughed. "I just want to know if he's gonna write something nice about Romero's. We could use the good press".

"I said as many nice things as possible. Davey—I mean, David—said that the article will probably run in a few days."

Soccoro leaned forward, her brows raised. "So? Are you going to his book reading?"

Adela stood and walked to the refrigerator. "I think we still have toppings for nachos, and I made pork belly tamales that I put away here. I'll get them out and warm them up. What did you ask me?"

Soccoro gave a soft humph. "His reading. You said he invited you."

"Oh, I don't know. I'm going to be busy with Romero's." Adela popped a pan of tamales in the oven.

"I'm not so old I can't take over for you for a few hours. And you're not too busy."

Adela avoided Soccoro's gaze. She didn't want to be pushed into a corner about anything right now— especially about Davey. She set dishes on the table and swung her gaze to the side. It landed on Richie. "Is Richie eating my lamb tamales?"

THE FOLLOWING MORNING, Sandra juggled a vase of flowers, her purse, and the keys to Romero's as she reached to insert the key to unlock the shop for the day. She breathed in deep of the flower-scented morning air. The pollen must have tickled her nose, and she sneezed.

"Need help?" a familiar male voice asked.

She looked over her shoulder, and her heart skipped a beat. "Victor. How are you?" She thrust the flowers at him. "Will you hold these?"

He grasped the vase. "From an admirer? You didn't go hang out in the produce department after all, did you?"

"Hardly." She unlocked and opened the front door. A burst of cool air washed over her. She turned to face him. "Thanks for the help. What brings you by?"

He chuckled and dipped his chin. "I promise I'm really not stalking you."

"You realize that's what all stalkers say." She shot him a sassy grin. "You want to come in?"

He looked down at a bag of groceries he held in one hand and shrugged. "These should be okay for a little bit."

"The diner is air conditioned, or if you'd like, you can put them in our fridge." She walked through the space and headed toward the kitchen where natural light shone in from a wall of windows.

"Thanks, but I can't stay long. I wanted to hear what your grandmother thought about things."

So that's why he was here. "Would you like a drink?" She moved behind the counter and reached for a cup. She started every shift here with a mix of sweet and unsweetened iced tea.

"Sure. Water's fine."

She filled a cup with ice and water and handed it to him. "To be honest, I was dismayed with her response." Though a twinkle lit her abuela's eyes, she seemed disappointed things had gone so well. Sandra had wanted to quiz her and find out why, but she was afraid to hear her response. She liked Victor and didn't want Abuela to spoil that.

"Did you ask her what was up?"

She shook her head. "She seemed happy for me, but I didn't have the nerve to dive into the deep end with her. All I can think of is she wants to be responsible for finding the man of my dreams."

"I see. That's too bad. I know you hoped for a better reaction." He took a sip of water and looked at the floor. "There's something else I wanted to talk to you about."

"What's that?"

He met her gaze. "Manny."

"Uh-oh. What about him?"

"Don't ask me how he knew where I lived, but he was waiting for me outside in my driveway this morning."

"Why?"

"He has it in his head that if he's working for your biggest competitor, then you'll have to hire him back with a raise. I thought you should know."

Sandra closed her eyes, took in a cleansing breath, and then let it out. "I'm really sorry he's dragged you into our drama. Manny told my aunt that he would not be returning. I think it's for the best. She's talking about selling anyway."

"Selling?" Victor's voice rose a notch. "But this place has been here forever."

"I know. Thirty years to be exact." The conversation she'd heard between Tía Soccoro and Patrick still hurt. Her aunt clearly didn't see her as someone capable of running Romero's. But why? She'd done a good job but clearly not good enough. She had her work cut out for her if she was going to convince Tía Soccoro she could manage this place.

"Thirty years is a long run," Victor said. "Your aunt could sell this place for enough money to retire comfortably, assuming she owns the building."

"She does." Was she being selfish, wanting her aunt to turn Romero's over to her? Tía Soccoro worked hard and deserved a comfortable retirement without the added worry of running a business they couldn't get out of the red. "Thanks for letting me know about Manny. I assume you still aren't interested in hiring him?"

Victor shook his head. "Not a chance. I don't want a man like that working for me. His attitude and scheming aside, it unnerved me that he searched out my home."

"Understandable. I'd feel the same way."

He tapped the counter and raised his cup to her. "I need to head out. Stop by the truck sometime. I want you to try something."

"But you're the competition. What will our customers think if they see me over there?"

"They'll think you support local businesses. Besides, we're friends. Friends taste test for each other." He picked up his bag of groceries and walked out.

A pan banged into something in the kitchen. Sandra whirled around. "Adela! I didn't realize you were here." How had she missed noticing her cousin-in-law?

"I see that. Your friend is cute." A knowing look filled her eyes.

"I agree, but we are just friends."

Adela glanced up from chopping peppers. "I didn't suggest otherwise."

"Victor owns the food truck that parks around the corner. What are you doing here so early?"

"I wanted to try out some new recipes." Adela placed a jalapeño pepper onto the cutting board and diced it like the pro she was. "Why was Victor here?"

She explained about Manny.

"That man has a lot of nerve."

"No kidding, but it doesn't change the fact we still need a cook."

Adela stopped chopping and looked up. "What am I?"

"A chef who's passing through. We both know you're not going to be here forever."

Adela returned her attention to the knife in her hand and diced an onion. "Forever is impossible to predict."

"I suppose." Sandra turned toward the dining area. "I need to get things ready for the lunch rush." She hated that Adela was right. How could anyone predict the future with one-hundred-percent accuracy? There was no way to know what tomorrow would hold. She stuffed napkins into the holder beside the cash register.

Was she doing the right thing hoping that someday Tía Soccoro would see her value and consider her a viable option for running this place? Or would it be better to stop focusing on Romero's and find another dream? Had Anthony been right? Did she have the position here because she was the only person in the family who wanted the job?

A shudder ran through her body. Surely, Tía Soccoro recognized the value she brought to Romero's even if she didn't consider her good enough to run the place. She shook away her thoughts and finished prepping for the lunch crowd. Then she flipped the sign on the window to open.

Word must have gotten out that a famous TV chef was cooking because as soon as she flicked on the dining room lights, people began to stream in. Her stomach lurched. Would they have enough food? She prayed so. Adela knew what she was doing. She'd worked here before becoming a famous chef. Sandra breathed a little easier at the thought as she greeted her next customer with a smile.

Around one o'clock business slowed. "I'm going to take a walk and get some air," Sandra said.

Tía Soccoro nodded, ginning wide. "You might want to rest your feet. If the dinner crowd was anything like the lunch crowd, we're going to be hopping."

"I'll keep that in mind." Sandra strolled out the door with no planned destination. Hot air warmed her almost too much. Maybe a walk wasn't her best idea, but she needed to escape the confines of Romero's. Adela being there changed the vibe, not necessarily in a bad way, but Sandra needed a break from the celebrity.

She turned the street corner and spotted Victor sitting at a portable picnic table in the shade of his food truck. A zip of excitement shot through her. What was that about? Victor was her competition, but he was such a nice man, and he had turned into a friend. His orange T-shirt hugged his body. The man clearly worked out. "Hey, Victor." She stopped beside the table.

He did a double take and stood. "This is a surprise. I didn't think you ever walked this direction."

She chuckled. "I don't normally. How's it going?"

His brown eyes held a hint of sadness. "Kind of slow today. How about you?"

"I'm sorry to hear that." She meant it too. Though she wanted Romero's to succeed, she didn't want Victor's business to fail. He worked so hard. "We had a surprisingly busy lunch crowd." The busiest she could remember.

He grinned and motioned to the seat across from where he had been sitting.

She sat, noting the heavy foot traffic coming in and out of the ice cream shop. This location was actually great if he capitalized on the surrounding businesses.

"Congratulations! It sounds like Adela is drawing a crowd."

That's what worried her. Once Adela moved on then what would happen? "I'm sure you're right, plus she's also revamping the menu. I think word is out, and people want to try her creations. I hate to admit it, but they're really good."

"Why do you hate to admit it?" He planted his elbow on the table and rested his chin on his fist.

"I don't think it's sustainable to serve what she's making. We'll go broke. She made lamb! Do you have any idea how expensive that is?"

"What does your aunt say?"

"She adores her daughter-in-law. In her eyes, Adela can do no wrong. My aunt has told her we can't afford those kinds of foods, yet she still makes them." Sandra couldn't believe she just told him all of that. There was something about Victor that caused her to lower her inhibitions.

Based on Adela's reaction to the kitchen, maybe they should've sunk money into revamping the kitchen and menu with only a modest refresh in the front house. They probably could have attracted an exceptional chef if they'd updated the kitchen.

"That's too bad about the expense," Victor said. "I'd love to try the lamb. Maybe I should add it to my menu. It can't be that expensive if I cut the slices thin and adjust the prices to reflect the meat choice."

"You might be right." Why hadn't she thought of that? She was supposed to be a business woman. It was her job to come up with innovative ideas. "So long as the quality of the food reflects the price, people would pay a little more."

"I know I would." Victor stood. "You want iced tea?"

He remembered. Her heart warmed at his thoughtfulness. She really needed to stay away from Victor. It would be way too easy to fall for him and that simply wasn't an option.

"Sure, thanks." She stood and walked to the window of the food truck as he went inside. "Mmm. It really smells good in there." Her stomach rumbled. They had been so busy she hadn't eaten lunch, and she'd neglected to pack one today.

Victor dumped peppers and onions onto the grill and then added pre-cooked chicken. "I want you to try my latest creation." He blocked her view so she couldn't see what else he was doing.

She angled to get a better view but still couldn't see what he was putting on the grill. "Afraid I'll steal your secrets?" Though she knew her way around a kitchen, she wasn't a master cook like Adela or apparently Victor.

He glanced over his shoulder. "Can't be too careful." He winked and turned back to the grill.

Her breath caught. Why did he have to be so handsome? "I would never steal your secrets. To be honest, cooking isn't one of my talents. I follow recipes fine but being creative with food not so much."

"I'm sure you have other talents." He turned and presented her with a street soft-taco and a large iced tea. An eager look rested on his face. "Be honest and tell me what you think? I've been tweaking the spices."

She took a bite and an explosion of flavor filled her mouth. Her eyes widened. "It's delicious! I can't believe you don't have a line wrapped around the block."

"I haven't served it yet."

When he did, Romero's was sure to go under. They had nothing with this much flavor and the perfect amount of heat on their menu—at least not yet. Maybe Adela would create something equally as exciting. Sandra took another bite and closed her eyes. "Victor, you must put this on your menu. I know we're competitors, and I'm probably killing Romero's by encouraging you, but this is *perfecto*."

His brow lifted. "Seriously? You think it's good enough."

She plopped the rest into her mouth then washed it down with the tea, which also tasted pretty good, and swallowed. "You're sitting on a gold mine. I wish you'd come work for Romero's. With your recipes and our history, we'd be a huge success."

"I appreciate the offer, but I like working for myself."

"I understand. What do I owe you?"

He waved his hands in the air. "You were a taste tester. No charge."

"Thanks. If you need anything else tested, I'm your girl."

"I'll keep that in mind." He nodded to something behind her.

She turned and saw a man waiting. "Oh, sorry." She stepped aside. "See you around, Victor." Tea in hand, she headed back to work. A tinge of worry niggled the back of her mind. Victor had stepped up his game to compete with Adela. What would they do when she left?

# Chapter Fifteen

ADELA SANK INTO A CHAIR AT Romero's during a slight lull later that day. The dining area had been packed with people an hour ago, with long lines at the counter and a server bringing out hot plates of the *"Especiales de Adela"* as displayed on the specials board...most prominent among them, Pork Belly Tamales. Adela had been working three hours straight and her feet throbbed. How had she done this years ago, day after day? She definitely wasn't getting any younger.

Soccoro wiped down the counter nearby and looked up when the bell on the door jingled. "Patrick! Back so soon?"

"I read that article in *The Telegram*. Like everyone else who's been in here today, apparently." He waved at the group of customers exiting the front door. "A good day for you, Soccoro?"

She grinned. "I had it framed!" She gestured behind the counter to a framed newspaper article with the headline: "Something New is Cooking at Romero's."

"You're something else, Soccoro. Way to go on making this place a success. I knew you could do it."

Adela watched pink suffuse Soccoro's cheeks. *Interesting.*

Soccoro gestured to where Adela was sipping her coffee. "Thanks to Adela."

"It was a great article, yes, but it's you, who's been keeping this place going all these years." A warm smile stretched his lips.

Soccoro's blush deepened.

Patrick reached out and patted Soccoro's hand that rested on the counter. "Maybe now you can retire?"

Soccoro gave him an arch look. "You are awfully interested in my retirement."

"Maybe if you had more free time, you and I could get together outside of work."

"Ha! I don't need to retire for that. So, what's it gonna be? Bean burrito?"

"Actually, I want to try an Especiales de Adela."

Adela slipped from her chair and headed back to the kitchen. Time to get to work...but she'd have to mull over that conversation soon.

Soccoro appeared at the kitchen window with an order slip, placed it in the clip, and then spun it to face Adela. One takeout order with all three specials.

"Can you believe all the customers we've had today?" She peered through the server window. "And more just came in. Wow!" Adela flew into high speed, thankful she had a skilled prep cook. "Fabi, nice job on keeping up with the dishes. You're about caught up."

Sandra unloaded fresh groceries into the fridge. "The article only came out yesterday. Let's wait and see if we still have as many customers this time next week."

"I know. I know. But still, it's exciting, isn't it? People

really like the new dishes." Adela filled the order for Patrick and handed it through the serving window to Soccoro.

"I suppose," Sandra said. "But I don't like how much we're spending on groceries. If this plan doesn't pan out, we need to consider raising prices if we are going to continue like this."

Soccoro pushed open the swinging door into the kitchen. "Hey, Adela! Look who's here."

Adela turned to see Soccoro gesture David inside. Adela's heart gave an unexpected flutter. What was wrong with her that she reacted so crazy every time David showed up lately?

"Get him the especiales. From now on, David eats on the house."

David shook his head. "Thanks, Soccoro. But I'm pretty sure that would violate my journalistic integrity." He smiled at Adela. "It's hard turning down such fantastic food, but I need to keep my reputation spotless, you know."

"Suit yourself." Soccoro gave Adela a wink and then headed back into the dining room.

David leaned a hip against the doorframe. "I do want to try the especiales. But I'm paying."

"What about our *elote*?" Adela shot him a grin. This man was so hard to act normal around.

"Ha! I'm getting that too."

She placed a hot pork belly tamale on a plate and garnished it. Then she scooped a generous helping of rice and beans next to it. "You must have a lot of fans, Davey.

It seems like half of San Antonio has been in here the past two days."

"They're your fans, not mine. I just wrote the article." He gave her a soft smile that made her hands tremble.

She tore her gaze away and concentrated on her work. She garnished the *chicharrón* nachos and started to pour ketchup on them but then grabbed the salsa bottle. *Get a grip, girl.*

"So, I was wondering... My reading's in a couple of days."

The reading. Right... She checked on a deep-frying chalupa shell that was turning black. She snatched it out of the fryer and flipped it onto a cooling rack. "I don't know. It's so hectic here. I'm not sure I'll have time to get away."

"It'll only be an hour or so. Most of my friends are chefs, so it's in the mid-afternoon between lunch and dinner."

"Hmm. I suppose it might work during that time period." She placed an avocado on her cutting board and started slicing it, but the knife almost grazed her fingers. Deliberately setting it down, she turned and gave David her full attention. She didn't need a trip to the ER from being careless with extremely sharp knives.

"I'd really appreciate if you came. I'm pretty nervous. I hate public speaking."

"Just act confident whether you're feeling it or not."

"I'll keep that in mind... So, what do you think?"

She wiped her hands on her apron, trying to gather

her composure. "I can't make any promises. Romero's is my top priority right now."

David straightened. "Hey, say no more. It's okay."

Adela finished his order. "Were you eating any of this here, or did you want it to go?"

"To go would be great, thanks."

She took a moment to bag up the full order and handed two bags to him. "This is on the house. I won't tell anyone, promise."

"Journalistic integrity, remember?" He handed her a few bills and took the bags. David opened up one of the bags and took out the pork belly tamale. He took a bite. A smile sprang to his lips.

Adela put her hands on her hips and tipped her head to one side. "As good as the elote?"

"Even better." He took another bite. "Take care, Adela, and thank you...for everything."

"You too, Davey."

Soccoro passed David in the doorway as he left the kitchen. She paused by Adela's workstation. "Adela, I was thinking..."

Adela looked up, but her mind was still on the man who'd just left her kitchen. She felt a bit dreamy inside, and she had to shake herself to pull out of it. "Yes?"

"What would you say to a little celebration tonight? In honor of all this success?

"I'd say that Sandra was right earlier. We probably shouldn't count our tamales before they cook."

"Oh, stop! That's ridiculous—we had a wonderful day today, and that's worth celebrating. Besides, even if we are only the flavor of the week, that doesn't mean it's not worth a fiesta. Fabi! Sandra!"

Fabiola turned her head from her wash station, and Sandra came around the corner and stopped a few feet away.

Soccoro waved an expressive hand in the air. "Girls, we're celebrating tonight at my house."

"Fun! I'm game." Sandra gave a half-smile, one of the first real smiles Adela had seen on her face since she'd started working at Romero's.

Fabi clapped her hands. "I'm in! Sounds like fun."

"Adela?" Soccoro waved a hand in front of Adela's face. "You seemed to have been drifting since David came to get his food." Her eyes twinkled.

"Ha! Kind of like you were doing when Patrick picked up his food?" Adela grinned. "Sure, a party sounds fun. Let's do it."

A few hours later, Adela sat on the edge of her bed. It had been a long but satisfying day at the diner, and the thought of a party with her family tonight had given her renewed energy. Her phone pinged, and she plucked it off the night stand and then sighed. Matias again. She'd better deal with this now and not put it off again. "Hey, Matias."

"Hey? Hey! I don't hear from you in days, and all I get is hey?"

She closed her eyes for a few seconds before answering. "I'm sorry. I've been busy."

"I get that, Adela, but the network is tired of waiting. They need an answer."

"Well, I don't have one yet. I'm sorry."

"Do you know how many people would kill for the position you're in? You can't keep stringing them—and me—along."

"I know, and I'd love to say yes, but family comes first."

Soccoro's voice echoed through the door. "Niñas. Dinner's ready."

"Sorry, Matias, but I've got to go. I'll get back to you soon. 'Bye." Like the coward she was, she clicked off her phone before Matias started his typical verbal storm.

# Chapter Sixteen

AFTER WORK, SANDRA ZIPPED HOME TO get ready for the party at Tía Soccoro's. It had been a long time since she'd attended a party at her aunt's house. Sandra rushed inside. "I'm home, Abuela!" She raced to her bedroom, quickly changed out of her work clothes, and then slipped into shorts and a T-shirt.

"Why are you in such a hurry?" Abuela stood in the doorway to her bedroom. "Do you have another date?"

"Not tonight. I'm going to a party at Tía Soccoro's to celebrate what a great day we had." She couldn't believe how excited she was about the party. They weren't really her thing but being included in the invite had felt like such a victory with her aunt that she couldn't help but feel happy about going.

"Humph. One day of success and you have a party? Such nonsense." Abuela crossed her arms. "I thought we were going to watch a movie together."

Sandra stopped moving and looked over at her grandmother. "How about we watch it tomorrow instead?"

Abuela frowned. "I've been waiting all day to watch it with you." She turned and walked away.

Guilt pressed in on Sandra. If anyone needed a man

in her life, it was her grandmother. She was lonely and relied too much on Sandra for companionship. What was she supposed to do? She loved her grandmother and wanted to please her and be around for her, but she could also be smothering. With a sigh she followed after the older woman. "Abuela, please don't be like this. How often have I cancelled on our movie night?"

Abuela paused before sitting in her favorite chair. "Never."

Sandra grinned. "That should count for something." She knelt in front of her grandmother and wrapped her hands over Abuela's. "If you want to watch the movie without me, I'll understand. You shouldn't have to wait an extra day for something you've been looking forward to because of me."

Abuela's frown lines softened. "I'll wait. It's not as much fun without you. I have some crocheting I can do. It's fine. Go have fun."

Relief filled Sandra. "Thank you." She stood and kissed her grandmother's forehead. "If you change your mind, I'll understand. Maybe Peter from next door would like to watch with you. I imagine he gets lonely since he lives alone."

Abuela jutted out her chin. "I'll be fine. I don't need our neighbor to keep me company."

"Of course not, but maybe he needs a friend." She held her breath. If Peter and Abuela got friendly, maybe she would relax a little and not be so persnickety and demanding of Sandra.

"I'll think about it."

Sandra nearly pumped a fist in the air. It wasn't a complete win, but when Abuela said she'd think about something, it meant she didn't hate the idea. This could be a game changer for both of them. Peter seemed to be a nice man. A widower for the past ten years, he had to be lonely. He'd offered more than once to stop in and check on Abuela when she was at work, but she'd always politely thanked him and never took him up on the offer.

"Why are you so set on going to this party? I thought you didn't like Adela."

Sandra froze. "I never said that." Though if she were honest, she was more than a little jealous of the woman's success. She was ashamed of herself for that and had been working hard to not feel that way.

Abuela shrugged. "You didn't have to. Remember you are a strong woman. You are smart, and you can do anything you put your mind too."

Sandra grinned. "I tell myself almost those exact words every day."

"I know. You think I don't have ears?" She reached for the crochet hook and yarn sitting in a basket on the floor beside her chair. "You have fun tonight."

"Thanks." She hesitated. *"Te quiero."*

"I love you too. Now go before you're late."

Sandra rolled her eyes. "I won't be late. Did you eat dinner?"

"I'm not hungry."

"You need to eat." Sandra moved to the kitchen and pulled out leftover *porketta* roast, rice, and Greek salad from yesterday. After heating the food and plating it, she carried it over to Abuela.

"You're too good to me." She set aside her crocheting and reached for the plate. "I don't know how I'm going to eat all of this."

Sandra grinned. Abuela had a ferocious appetite. She only liked to pretend to eat like a bird. "Don't wait up. I'm not sure how late I'll be."

"Okay. Have fun."

"I will. Thanks." She headed out with a bounce in her step even after such a busy day.

Peter waved from his front yard. He held a hose over a freshly planted shrub. "Evening, Sandra. How's your grandmother?"

She glanced over her shoulder toward the door and strolled closer to the fence that divided their yards. She kept her voice low. "I think she could use some company. I was supposed to watch a movie with her tonight, but something came up."

"Oh. That's too bad." His brow furrowed. "Evie and I used to watch movies together on Saturday evenings." He chuckled. "They weren't my kind of shows, but they made her so happy."

"What did she like?" Peter had never talked about his wife to her.

"Romance and romantic comedy were her favorites."

"We were going to watch *Sleepless in Seattle*."

His face lit. "That's a good one." He glanced toward his house. "One of the church women brought by a peach pie. It's really too much for one person. Do you think your grandmother would enjoy a slice?"

Sandra grinned. This had worked out better than she'd imagined. "I know she would. Peach is one of her favorites. Have a good evening. I need to go."

"Yes, of course." He twisted the hose faucet off and then headed inside with a spring to his step.

Sandra shook her head and held in a giggle. "Well, that was interesting." It looked like she had inherited her grandmother's matchmaking, but Sandra wasn't so obvious about it.

# Chapter Seventeen

ADELA TOOK A HANDFUL OF POPCORN from a nearby bowl and tossed a few pieces into her mouth. She hadn't felt this relaxed in a long time. She looked around Soccoro's living room and smiled. Fabi and Soccoro were totally into the game of charades, but Sandra not so much. A frown marred her face as her fingers moved like they were turning pages in rapid succession.

Soccoro slapped her hand on her knee. "I know! She's filing papers. She's a secretary."

"No, she's scratching records." Fabi jumped to her feet and waved her arms in the air as though she'd scored a goal. "I've got it. She has to be a DJ!"

Sandra shook her head, her lips shut tight.

"Are you swimming? It has to be swimming." Soccoro cocked her head to the side and squinted her eyes.

An egg timer dinged on the nearby coffee table. Sandra groaned. "The word was chef. I was cooking. Beating stuff in a bowl, cracking eggs...you know, cooking?"

Confused expressions mirrored themselves on both Soccoro's and Fabi's faces. Adela stifled a laugh. She hadn't taken part in this round, but she hadn't caught the cooking symbolism either.

"No, that was not cooking. Maybe you should spend some more time in the kitchen, Sandra." Soccoro laughed.

Sandra flopped down onto the couch and reached for a fistful of popcorn. "Thanks a lot, guys. I thought it was pretty clear."

Soccoro pressed her lips together in an apparent effort to not laugh again. She reached down and stroked Richie who was asleep on the floor at her feet.

"Mom, you're next." Fabi snapped her fingers at Adela.

Adela pushed up from the couch and reached into a bowl on the coffee table filled with scraps of paper. "I can't remember the last time we all did this together. It's been a fun evening."

"I think it was at the going-away party before we left for L.A. Dad loved charades."

Sandra nodded and tossed a few more kernels of popcorn into her mouth. "He should've had the career in Hollywood."

Adela sighed and then smiled. "I won't argue with that."

"I do remember you being pretty bad, however." Sandra shot Adela a saucy grin.

"Yeah, but Dad could always guess what Mom was acting out. It was like they had a psychic connection or something." Fabi smiled, and Adela met her daughter's gaze, her own eyes growing moist. "Yeah. That was a fun party, for sure." Adela cleared her throat and read the word in her hand. "This is a tough one."

Fabi smirked. "You always say that."

Adela put her hands on her hips and shot her daughter a haughty glare. "Just wait until your turn, little smarty-pants. Okay, set the timer..."

An hour later, Sandra pushed to her feet. "Thanks for a great night, ladies. I'll see you early. *Manana*. I need a little shuteye so I can crawl out of bed in the morning."

Fabi yawned. "I'm going to bed too. 'Night." She walked over to her mom and grandmother, gave them each a hug, and then headed for her bedroom.

"She's such a sweet girl. You must be proud, Adela."

Adela choked up all over again, but this time from pride rather than her earlier longing for what she'd lost with her husband. "Yeah, she is."

Soccoro leaned forward and patted Adela's knee. "I overheard you today in the kitchen talking with David. Why don't you go to his reading?"

"I don't know. I guess I didn't think about it, but we're really too busy at the diner. I'd hate to leave you without anyone but the prep cook."

"Pfft. We'll figure out a way to cover you. David did us a big favor. And besides that, he's a nice guy, and I can tell you like him. You should go for his sake as well as for yours." A Cheshire-like smile pulled at Soccoro's lips.

Adela blinked a few times, trying to take in what she'd heard. "No, I don't! Not the way you're implying, anyway."

Soccoro sighed. "Adela—life goes on. You can't live in pain forever."

"I'm not."

"I know you miss my son...so do I. But you can't give

up on love. I want you to be happy, and Mauricio would want that too. You know he'd hate to see you and Fabi alone."

Adela bit her lip. Was Soccoro right? Had she given up on love—on being happy? "I don't know if I'm ready."

Soccoro nodded and then leaned over and drew Adela into a warm hug. "I understand. But at least think about it, all right? Don't rush to say no to the possibility, either."

"I have to get some sleep. Thank you for caring. You are one-in-a-million as far as mothers-in-law go."

*"Buenas noches."*

"And good night to you too, Richie."

A few minutes later, Adela climbed into bed. She stared at the photo of Mauricio on the nightstand and then turned off the lamp determined to put all thoughts of the past out of her mind and go to sleep. She had barely drifted into a doze, when a buzzing near her head jarred her awake. She reached out and checked her phone on the nightstand. Another call from Matias. Adela hesitated a moment and then let the call ring to voicemail. Time for that tomorrow. She'd dealt with enough today, and she needed this night to end on a happy note, not another argument with her agent.

# Chapter Eighteen

SANDRA BREEZED INTO ROMERO'S FROM THE kitchen and stopped short. Anthony stood at the counter. What was he doing here? She squared her shoulders and marched up to the cash register. "Sorry to keep you waiting."

"No problem. I was hoping we could talk."

"I'm working."

"Do you get a break?" Anthony asked.

What was up with this guy? After the things he'd said to her on their date, she couldn't imagine he'd have more to add. "I think you made your opinion of me quite clear. I see no reason for us to talk."

"I owe you an apology. I'm sorry for being such a jerk. It was wrong for me to judge you."

"Apology accepted." She looked past him to the woman waiting to place an order. "I'll be right with you." She looked back at Anthony. "I have *customers* to help."

"Right. Of course. I'd like the elote."

"Anything to drink?"

"Water, please."

"Your order will be right up." She quickly gave Adela his order and then returned to help her next customer.

"Order up," Adela said.

Sandra turned and pulled Anthony's street corn off the counter, placed it on a tray, and took it to him. "Enjoy. We are famous for our elote."

"I've heard. You sure you can't join me?"

The lunch crowd had thinned to almost nothing, and no one waited to place an order. It seemed talking to him would be the only way to get rid of him. She sighed. "Only for a minute." She sat and crossed her arms. When he dug into his corn without speaking, she almost walked away.

He looked up from his corn. "You got me into a lot of trouble with my grandmother."

"Seems to me you did that all by yourself."

He chuckled. "I like you, Sandra. You stand up for yourself, and you don't take garbage from people."

His words almost took her voice away. He gave her a compliment? Shocker. "Uh, thank you." Suspicion clouded her voice. What was he up to? "What do you want, Anthony? I might not know you well, but I know people, and you're up to something."

He nodded. "Guilty. My grandmother won't let our date drop. I'm hoping you'll give me a second chance."

She shook her head. "Why would I do that?"

"Because you're a nice person?" He raised a brow.

"I am, but I also don't see a future for us. Why pretend otherwise?"

"Then go out with me as a friend. Not a date."

She narrowed her eyes. What was with this guy? "We aren't friends."

"Yet." His smoldering gaze met hers.

She looked away. "I don't know. I'm pretty busy." If

she went out with him again, it would qualify as a date for her deal with Abuela since this technically wasn't a set up, but did she really want to spend more time with this man? Especially when Victor already asked her out for this week. She actually looked forward to watching his team play. Sure, there was next week, but if things went well with Victor, she'd hoped they'd find something else to do together so she wouldn't have to date another man like Anthony.

Anthony cleared his throat. "We can do anything you'd like. I'm free every night this week."

"I'm not. I promised my grandmother I'd watch a movie with her tonight."

"Perfect!" His face lit. "I'll join you."

"Are you *loco*? You can't meet my grandmother. She'll get her hopes up and think we're a thing. Her greatest wish in life is to see me happily married." Though, Abuela hadn't jumped to conclusions with Victor, she had a feeling seeing Anthony would be a different story.

He furrowed his brows. "I see the problem. How about another night? I could meet you here, and we could get ice cream at that shop around the corner."

She narrowed her eyes. "If I agree to have ice cream with you, will you leave me alone after that?"

"If that's what you want. I promise to never bother you again."

"Fine. We can get ice cream tonight, but it will have to be quick. No more than thirty minutes. I'll call my grandma and let her know I'll be a little late."

"That'll work. Thanks." He stood. "My compliments to the cook. The elote lived up to its reputation. See you later."

Soccoro sidled up to her and sat in the spot where Anthony had been. "He's handsome. New boyfriend?"

"No. Just some guy Abuela set me up with. He was horrible on our first date and stopped in to apologize. I agreed to have ice cream with him after my shift tonight."

"That's nice of you. You like him then?"

She thought for a second. "I don't know what I think of him. If you'd asked me that the day we went to brunch, I'd have said absolutely not. He was very rude." She suspected he never would have humbled himself to apologize if his grandmother hadn't made his life difficult.

Soccoro stood. "Trust your instincts. Just because he looks nice on the outside, doesn't mean he's nice on the inside. I don't want you to get hurt."

Her heart warmed. It felt good to be sincerely cared about. "I know. I'll be careful. It's only ice cream." Though impressed that he'd humbled himself to apologize even if it was to get his grandmother off his back, she doubted his opinion of her had changed. His grandmother must be even more difficult than hers.

AFTER HER SHIFT Sandra headed to the restroom to freshen up. She applied lipstick and blotted her face with blotting papers. She looked in the mirror and sighed. She should have told Anthony no. Going on a date at the end of a long day was no way to impress a man. She shook her head. Habits were hard to break. There was no need to impress him. As far as she was concerned, he needed to impress her. She raised her chin and left the restroom.

Anthony walked into Romero's as she strode out of the restroom. He raised a hand in greeting.

She strolled over to him. "Right on time."

"Being late is a pet peeve."

She laughed. "You and I are vinegar and water." What had Abuela been thinking? It was as if her grandmother didn't know her at all.

He held open the door for her, allowing her to precede him outside. "Why do you say that?"

"I'm only ever on time for work. Oh, and our date, but that was a fluke."

"Good to know."

She walked toward the ice cream shop which happened to be on the same block as Victor's food truck. "How was your day?"

"I hate talking about work."

"Okay." She drew out the word. Why had their grandmothers thought they would be a good match? They had to have seen something, but she was clueless as to what it could be. Their grandmothers clearly didn't know them as well as they thought. "What do you like to talk about?"

"Good question. I spend all day talking, so when I get home, I generally don't talk."

She rolled her eyes. "This should be interesting." She spotted Victor closing the window on his food truck.

Victor looked her way. His face broke into a huge smile. He glanced at Anthony, and his smile fled.

She caught her breath.

"Everything okay?" Anthony asked.

"Fine. Do you mind ordering for me? I need to talk to my friend really quick."

"Sure. What would you like?"

"A single scoop of mint chocolate chip on a sugar cone. Thanks. I'll be inside in a minute." She homed in on Victor and stopped beside his truck. She ducked her head inside. "How did it go today?"

Victor stepped out to join her on the sidewalk. "That your boyfriend?" He glanced toward the ice cream shop.

"You know I don't have a boyfriend. He was my brunch date."

"You're kidding? You gave him another chance?"

She shrugged. "He practically begged me after apologizing for what he said."

"You see a future with him?" Victor stared at the sidewalk.

She shook her head vehemently. "Not a chance. I only agreed to this to get him to leave me alone."

Confusion filled Victor's face. "How does that work?"

"I'll explain later. I don't have much time. I promised my grandmother I'd watch a movie with her tonight. I'm hoping to count this ice cream date as part of my deal with her. Not sure she'll go for it though since I technically have two dates in one week thanks to you." She flashed him her best smile.

He grinned. "Now I get it. Come by tomorrow. I have something else I want you to taste."

"Sure. See you." She turned and headed to the ice cream shop.

"Sandra," Victor called out.

She turned.

"Does your date tonight mean you won't be coming to the basketball game and dessert after?"

"Not a chance. I wouldn't miss your game, and I'm looking forward to dessert." She waved, turned, and went inside the ice cream shop. Anthony stood at the register with their cones. She walked over to him. "Looks like I have perfect timing."

"I'd say so. It's too cold in here. You want to sit outside?"

It didn't seem too cold to her, but it was a nice evening, so she didn't mind. "Sure"

He held the door. "After you."

"Thanks." She sat at the nearest table in the shade of an elm tree. One of the things she looked forward to most was getting off her feet after standing all day. A warm breeze rustled the leaves of the tree, creating a relaxing sound. "This is nice." She had the perfect view of Victor as he finished closing up his truck.

"Yeah." Anthony placed his phone on the table in front of him.

She licked her ice cream. "You're a vanilla man, I see."

He licked the melting treat before it hit the side of the cone. "Love it, but I change it up for chocolate now and then."

MIRALEE FERRELL and KIMBERLY ROSE JOHNSON

*Boring.* She smiled and took another lick. "What do you do for fun?"

"I like to play racquetball."

Too much work if you asked her. "What else?"

"Hmm. I enjoy trying out new restaurants."

"You're a foodie?" Surprise filled her voice.

"Why so surprised?"

"Vanilla ice cream is not all that adventurous."

His jaw set before he took another lick. "Be careful. Some people might accuse you of being judgmental."

"You have to admit I'm right. It doesn't get more ordinary than vanilla."

"Says the woman who clearly has never tried it from this shop." He held out his cone to her. "Go on and take a lick. I think you'll understand why I like it. Not all vanillas are equal. This one should win an award."

She licked the side, and her eyes widened. Okay, he might be onto something, but she'd never admit it. "It's pretty good, but it's no mint chocolate chip."

He chuckled. "Thanks for doing this. I needed a stress reliever."

"Ice cream has a way of making everything better." Including this *date.* She still wasn't crazy about Anthony, but he was growing on her. "Why'd you become a lawyer."

He shook his head. "Remember no work talk?"

"Right." She licked her ice cream, savoring the silence. He was the one who wanted to do this, he could carry the conversation if he wanted to talk.

Victor's food truck rumbled to life and then pulled

164

away from the curb. She missed him already. Her phone vibrated. She checked the caller ID. "It's my abuela. She's wondering when I'll be home. I should go." She stood. "Thanks for the treat."

He stood. "I'll walk you to your car."

She shook her head. "Not necessary."

"At least let me walk with you back to Romero's."

She shrugged and headed toward the sidewalk. "What are you going to tell your grandmother about us?" After further consideration, it didn't make sense to mention the ice cream date. Especially since it lasted all of ten minutes. As far as Abuela was concerned, Anthony was ancient history. Hopefully, Anthony's grandmother would let it drop and not mention it to her.

His arm brushed hers as they strolled toward Romero's. "That you're a nice woman but not for me."

"Diplomatic."

"I try. How about you? What will you tell your grandmother?"

"Nothing. She thinks I'm shopping for food. Which I still need to do." Sandra picked up her pace. It wouldn't take long to get what she needed to throw together dinner.

"You lied?"

"Of course not. I just left out the part about meeting you for ice cream. I wouldn't want to get her hopes up only to disappoint her. I think it's safe to say you and I are not a match."

"We could be."

She stared at him for a second. "You've got to be

kidding. You just said I'm not for you. Talk about whiplash." What was with this man? It seemed he had no idea what he wanted. Well, she knew what she wanted, and it wasn't him. She stopped at the driveway to Romero's. "Thanks for the ice cream. Best of luck with your love life." Without waiting for a response, she turned and hustled to her pickup with no regrets.

"I'M HOME." SANDRA nudged the door closed with her foot, kicked off her shoes, and then headed for the kitchen with the groceries. She stopped short as she left the entryway and sniffed the air. "Abuela? Did you cook? It smells like enchiladas."

"Sí. I figured you might not be feeling up to it after your *date*." Abuela stood in the kitchen wearing an apron and holding a potholder.

"How...?" She set the two grocery bags on the counter.

"My friend called."

Sandra closed her eyes. She should have thought of that. "I didn't tell you because I didn't want to get your hopes up. It was only a quick ice cream date. Then we parted ways. I took so long because I picked up groceries like I said I would."

Grandmother waved her potholder in the air. "You can always be completely honest with me. I'm a grown woman. I can take it. Besides, you can do better than a man who doesn't respect you."

"But don't you agree with him? You want me to leave Romero's too."

Abuela pulled a hot pan from the oven. "To have a family. Not because I don't think it's a worthy profession."

"I can have both if I want to." That wasn't how her grandmother had chosen to live her life, but Sandra was her own person. She wanted a career and if a family happened then great, but if not, then that was fine too.

"Enough talking. Let's eat." Abuela placed a scoop of Spanish rice onto two plates and added an enchilada beside each mound.

"Gracias. I wish you would have told me you were cooking. I wouldn't have stopped at the store." She quickly put her purchases away. The food would keep for another day.

"I wanted to surprise you. But you get to clean the kitchen."

"Of course." She resisted rolling her eyes and sat at the kitchen table.

Abuela bowed her head.

Sandra said a silent blessing for her meal and then dug in. She was a little sick of Mexican food, but at least she hadn't had to cook. "Maybe you should tell Tía Soccoro you want to take over as the head cook at Romero's. No one makes Mexican food the way you do."

"Gracias, mi amor, but this old woman is not interested in cooking for strangers."

"What movie are we watching tonight? Did you still want to watch *Sleepless in Seattle*?"

"Actually, I watched it last night." Abuela focused on her food and avoided eye contact.

"Really? Did Peter happen to stop by with pie?"

Abuela's gaze slammed into hers. Her face flushed. "How did—?"

"We talked on my way out last night. He asked if you liked peach pie. How was the pie?"

"I make better."

Sandra ducked her chin to hide her smile. "Of course, you do. Did he stick around for the movie?"

"Well, yes. I had to invite him in. It would have been rude to send him on his way."

Sandra nodded and scooped a big bite of enchilada into her mouth.

Abuela waved her fork at Sandra. "Don't you gloat. I see what you did. You set me up."

"Me?" Sandra widened her eyes in mock horror. "I don't know what you're talking about. I only had a friendly conversation with our neighbor on my way out."

"Bah!" Abuela stuffed a bite of rice into her mouth.

Sandra chuckled. "Do you still want to watch a movie?"

"Sí. I picked out a couple of classics. You can decide which one."

"Thanks." Abuela usually choose what they watched. Maybe Peter had already rubbed off on her. She'd suspected for a couple of months now that the man might be interested in her grandmother. Especially since he always asked about her if he spotted Sandra outside. She shook away her thoughts and glanced at her grandmother.

Abuela watched her eagerly.

She blinked. "Did I miss something?"

"No, but I do have something to tell you."

"Uh-oh. Now it all makes sense. The meal, letting me choose the movie. What did you do?" At least she could rest assured it wasn't another date since she'd been sticking with her end of their deal.

"I might have set you up on another blind date."

"What!" Sandra's food soured in her stomach. "We talked about this. You promised! We made a deal." She'd trusted Abuela. "How could you?"

"It couldn't be helped. This man is perfect for you."

Sandra shook her head. "I don't know how you meet all these men when you never leave the house."

Abuela's eyes widened. "I leave the house every day. Just because I'm here when you leave and come home, doesn't mean I spend the entire day in my chair."

Now *this* was news. "I shouldn't have assumed. I'm sorry, but I'm not going on any more blind dates. I've kept up my end of our deal. You can't break the rules."

Abuela crossed her arms. "He's one of the good ones. Trust me."

"Like I did with Anthony? I don't think so." She stood, rinsed her plate, and then washed and set it in the rack on the counter.

Abuela sidled up beside her and washed her own plate. "Anthony was a mistake. I *met* this man at the butcher shop. You will like him."

"No. Call him and tell him I'm not coming." Her grandmother had lost her scruples if she thought this was going to happen. She reached for the three movies beside the TV and chose an old black and white without even reading the title. It was only ninety minutes long.

Abuela sank into her chair. "I don't have his number."

"What? Why not? Why would you set me up with a man and not get his contact information?"

"I know where he works." She shrugged. "Now hush. The movie is starting."

"Fine. We can talk after." Sandra tucked her legs and snuggled into the couch. She did her best to concentrate on the movie, but her mind raced. She hated standing up the man, but it looked to be her only option. Her grandmother had gone too far this time, and she needed to be the one to fix it if she really cared about this man's feelings.

# Chapter Nineteen

DAVID'S GAZE ROAMED THE GROWING CROWD on the rooftop of the restaurant overlooking the Riverwalk and tried to still his jittering nerves. He managed to write a column or do an interview with no problems—but stand up in front of two or three dozen people and tell them about his book and why he wrote it? He shuddered and set his coffee to the side. It would be a good idea not to have anything unnecessary on his stomach until this evening had ended. If only he could get through it without being sick or making a fool of himself. He'd honestly hoped no one would show—after all, he wasn't a big name, and this was his first book, but it appeared his friend Julio had helped spread the word.

Julio wandered over from the buffet holding a variety of Tex-Mex dishes along with several beverages and held up his drink in a solemn toast. "This is your big day, Davey. Are you excited?" He glanced at David's empty hands. "Where's your drink?"

David plucked his cup of coffee off the sideboard where he'd placed it and met Julio's toast. "Thanks, man. I appreciate your help and support." He gave his friend a weak smile. "There's more people than I expected, though."

"Hey, how often does your buddy write a book? The food community wants to support you. You've been a champion for us. We're here to return the favor."

David tried to relax and managed a small smile that felt more like a grimace. "I appreciate it. I'm just used to writing, not speaking."

Julio slapped his back. "You'll be fine."

David scanned the crowd again, hoping his friend knew what he was talking about, but right now his mind felt numb and not a thing he'd memorized came to mind. He fingered his notes in his pocket. He'd hoped not to need them—to come across as polished and self-assured, but somehow it didn't appear that was going to happen.

Thirty minutes later, David held a copy of his book while he stood in front of the crowd at a little mic. The gathering had continued to grow, and most of the chairs were filled. He cleared his throat, desperately wanting to wipe the sweat from his forehead. "Welcome everyone..." He pulled at his collar and glanced out at the audience. A few people raised eyebrows and others whispered. Panic stole through David's brain and nearly froze his tongue to the roof of his mouth.

The click of heels tapped across the floor at the back of the room, and David turned his attention that direction, dreading to see even one more person coming to stare at him while he fumbled through his speech.

Adela slipped into a seat about three rows from the front and flashed an apologetic smile at David. She held up two thumbs, grinned, and then mouthed the words, "You've got this."

David drew in a calming breath, stuffed his notes back into his pocket, and opened his mouth as the rabbits that had been bouncing from one part of his insides to the other lay down to take a nap. "I think you all know I'm a lot more comfortable behind a laptop than a microphone. Or even better, behind a plate at a local restaurant."

A rumble of quiet laughter floated across the audience.

David grinned, his confidence growing. "But seriously, I'm honored to see so many friends from San Antonio's food community here today. I'm such a fan of yours, it means the world to me that you would give up part of your evening to support me." He glanced at Adela who nodded and gave him another thumbs up.

With a smile, David cracked open his book. "I'll just read a few paragraphs to give you a *taste* of what's in store for you if you decide to take one of these books home. Then I'll tell you a little about how I came to write it."

Cheers and applause rang across the room as Adela and David made eye contact. She quirked a brow at him and tipped her head to the side.

A half hour later, David stood by his table of books, chatting and signing copies for people waiting in line. Adela moved up as the person ahead of her tucked his book under his arm and walked away. "I'm surprised you made it."

"I talked to the boss, and she told me I should come. Apparently, she felt they could handle the diner for a couple of hours without me."

"Well, I'm glad you're here. When you walked in

and gave me the thumbs up, it felt like everything inside settled down and calmed. Thank you for that."

"You were great. I don't know why you were so nervous. You were a natural up there, both with your reading and sharing your story." She picked up one of his books. "How much? I can't possibly leave here without a copy."

"How 'bout you just plug me on *Alta Cocina* sometime?"

Adela handed him the book. "Only if you sign it for me, and not just your name."

David's heart jumped. Dare he say something personal? Like he'd waited for her for years and wondered if there was any hope for them? He shook the thought away. She was still grieving her husband even though it had been three years. He wouldn't be that crass or pushy. He scribbled a lame note about being glad they'd renewed their friendship and handed it back.

She took it but didn't look inside before tucking it under her arm. "How about you come on and plug it yourself?"

"I don't know if I'm quite ready for TV yet, but thanks for the offer. Tonight was nerve-wracking enough."

"If you say so..."

"Adela. Hey!" Julio swooped over and greeted Adela. A couple more of David's foodie friends, Helen and Bart, strolled in his wake and then came to a stop behind him.

"Hey, Julio! Long time no see. How've you been?"

"Adela Romero remembers my name! I think I'm gonna faint." He placed the back of his hand across his forehead and swayed on his feet.

Adela laughed and punched him on the shoulder. Then she stepped aside as David came around the table. "Guys, meet Adela. Adela, Bart owns a Modern Peruvian restaurant downtown, and Helen manages San Antonio's best Mezcal bar. You and Julio are obviously acquainted."

"I adore *Alta Cocina*." Helen's warm brown eyes sparkled as she extended her hand to Adela.

"Wow, thanks!"

Bart reached out and shook her hand next. "And I'm loving that new pork belly tamale at Romero's. I could eat there every day, but I can't let my customers see that."

Julio laughed. "Yeah, better not. But I hear you. Everyone's talking about that dish."

"It's great to see you make that place come alive again." Bart took a drink of his coffee and then set the cup on the end of the table.

David nodded, wanting to show Adela how much he'd appreciated her support in showing up, and hoping she'd realize he meant every word. "Not to mention give every cook in town some more competition. Adela is an amazing cook."

Bart grinned. "That too!"

"You have such a supportive food scene here." Adela said. "I'm glad I've been able to reacquaint myself. It's nice to see you all come together tonight for David."

Helen waved manicured nails in the air. "Normally, I never trust a critic, but David's one of the good ones."

"I'm finding that out." Adela shared a private glance with David.

"I'm going to go hit the buffet again. Anyone want to join me? The food tonight is fabulous." Helen waved toward the thinning crowd near the buffet table.

Adela seemed to hesitate. "Actually...I can't stay."

Disappointment hit David hard. He'd been hoping she'd stick around, and they'd have time to talk, but at least she'd made the effort to come. Maybe she had a date with someone she planned to meet after she left here. "I'm sorry to hear that. The diner's not still open this late, is it?"

"No." Adela glanced at her watch. "But my daughter is playing with this pickup soccer team tonight, and I wanted to watch their game."

David's spirit soared. "Sounds like fun. I think I mentioned before that I enjoy soccer."

"I'd invite you to come along, but you have your party. I don't think you can abandon all your guests."

David looked around the patio at the partygoers. "A few of them have already left, and it looks like the ones that are left are headed for the bar, which doesn't interest me in the slightest. They can go on without me. I'd rather go with you and watch Fabi play soccer if you meant what you said."

ADELA STOOD NEXT to David, her gaze scanning the small crowd in the soccer stands. Since this wasn't an official school or team game, it appeared it was mostly parents and a few friends scattered across the stands.

David nudged her arm. "Up there." He pointed to the third from the top bleacher at Sandra and Soccoro. "It doesn't look like they've seen us yet, but there's plenty of room next to Soccoro if you want to go up?"

Adela nodded. "Perfect. I was hoping it wouldn't be too crowded so we could sit with them. It looks like the game just started. I'm so glad we didn't miss much. I've missed way too many of Fabi's games in the past, and I know this one is important to her."

David arched his brows but didn't reply, just put his hand under her elbow and guided her up the steps.

Why had she said so much to him? It seemed like every time she was around this man, she wanted to share her heart with him, and that was plain stupid. He wouldn't be interested in her interactions with her daughter or the mess she'd made of their relationship, and the last thing she wanted was for him to think of her as a terrible mother.

"Hey, look." David stopped her before they got near the top. He pointed. A young man who appeared to be Fabi's age, saved the ball from scoring a goal by the other team. Then he punted the ball back to Fabi. She worked it down the field, dribbling and then passing it to a teammate. Soccoro's voice rose above the rest. "Go, Fabi! You've got this!"

Adela grinned as she made her way to the empty spot next to her mother-in-law and sank down beside her, patting the spot on her other side for David. "Hey, guys. We made it. I told Fabi I wouldn't stay long at the book signing but look who decided to come with me."

Soccoro leaned around Adela. "Hey, David. Glad you could make it and you dragged this young woman back here in time so she didn't miss the game."

Sandra waved from Soccoro's other side. "We just got here too. The game's only been going for about five minutes."

"Romero's was a zoo again. All thanks to David." Soccoro tossed a smile at David. "His reviews have been bringing the customers in every day."

"It's not my reviews; it's Adela's cooking. But I'm gonna have to review those especiales soon. Everyone's buzzing about the new tamale."

"For now." Sandra's voice penetrated even in the chatter around them.

"*A qué te refieres?*" David stared at her.

Sandra shrugged. "Adela's doing a great job in the kitchen, but when she leaves, the customers might too. It's not like she's going to stay here forever."

"Don't be so negative, Sandra. Adela set us up for success." Soccoro's tone was good humored but had a slight scold to it as well.

"I hope you're right." Sandra shot Adela a stern look and then returned to watching the game.

"Well on that happy note, how about we turn our attention to the star of this evening, Fabi." Adela drew in a deep breath. "Go, Fabi! Your team is looking good, girl!"

David nudged Adela. "Look, Fabi has a breakaway!" They all turned their attention to the field as Fabi went one-on-one with the opposing team's goalie. She kicked the ball. The goalie dove, arms spread for the block. The ball whizzed past him. Score! Everyone around Adela jumped up and cheered. Fabi jogged past, smiling at everyone—then she lifted her hand and waved at Adela.

David raised his voice above the din. "You have a very talented daughter. She acts like she owns that field and knows exactly what to do every minute."

"I know. Soccer is her passion. I'm so glad she found a team to play with here." She gave David a shy smile as they settled back down to watch the rest of the game, and in spite of herself, warmth spread through her as his arm brushed hers.

FABI HIGH-FIVED Brandon and the other players on their team after their exciting win. She'd met Brandon first, but she'd been getting better acquainted with the other kids and hadn't met anyone she didn't like. Pretty cool to have a team with so much support who enjoyed having fun as much as they loved winning.

She hurried over to her family who waited on the sidelines. It was so amazing to have her mom here for an entire game. She could barely remember the last time that had happened. "Hey, everyone. Thanks for coming."

Abuela reached out and drew her into a hug. Fabi would never get tired of those hugs. "Way to go, Fabi! You were awesome, baby."

Sandra nodded. "Yeah. It was cool seeing you help make that goal, and great the way your team plays so well together. Congratulations!"

"Thanks..." Her eyes moved from her mother to

David. She'd met him a couple of times now, and he'd said he loved soccer, but why had he come to her game? Was he already here and bumped into her mom and grandmother? "Hey."

"Fabi, you remember Davey? I mean, David. Sorry." Mom gestured to the guy standing next to her, looking way too comfortable. They hadn't been holding hands, had they?

Fabi tipped her head toward David. "Hey. What are you doing here?"

"Fabi! That sounded rude." Abuela shook her finger at Fabi.

"Sorry." She scuffed her toe on the grass, but she wasn't going to take back the question. She wanted to know.

David extended his hand to her, and Fabi hesitated. He wanted to shake hands? That was just weird. She held out her fist. He grinned and then gave her a knuckle bump. So maybe he wasn't totally weird. "It was an honor watching you play. You're like a young Alex Morgan."

Fabi stifled a small gasp. "You know Alex Morgan? She's my favorite player!"

"A little secret if you promise not to tell anyone so I don't lose my reputation as a food critic—I love soccer almost as much as I love food."

Fabiola grinned. She might end up liking this guy. "Are you and my mom dating or something?"

"Fabi! What kind of a question is that?" Mom put her hand over her heart as though Fabi had shocked her, but Mom had asked her embarrassing questions in front of her friends more than once.

She shrugged. "Just wondering."

"As I know you're aware, David has been very kind in his reviews of the diner. I felt I owed it to him to support him at his book signing tonight. He mentioned how much he loves soccer when I told him I needed to leave early, and I told him he was welcome to come."

Fabi turned wide eyes on David. "You left your book signing to come see me play? Seriously?"

David tipped his head to the side. "It was almost over, but I'd had as much as I could take of the schmoozing and small talk. Getting out into the fresh air sounded like a good idea, so I tagged along with your mom. I hope you don't mind?"

Did she? She thought about it for a minute and then shook her head. "Nope. Not at all. I'm kind of glad Mom has a cute guy to hang out with." She shot him a grin and then turned to stare at her mom.

Color flooded Mom's cheeks. "We'd better head home for dinner. You must be starving, Fabi."

"Adios, David! We'll see you at the diner soon." Soccoro waved and then nudged Sandra toward the car.

Fabi walked backward so she could keep an eye on her mother and David. "See you later, David." She dragged her feet through the grass, determined to stay within earshot of her mother.

David's voice carried clearly on the still air. "Thanks for inviting me tonight."

"Thanks for ditching your party for to watch a kids' soccer game."

Fabi stiffened. Had Mom forced this guy to come? Maybe she didn't like him after all.

"I had fun. Trust me. I meant it when I told Fabi I love soccer, and she's an amazing player. Like I said, your daughter has talent."

"I agree, and I had fun too." Mom's voice was softer, and Fabi had to strain to hear, but her heart swelled at the praise from both of them.

David's voice grew softer as well, and Fabi slowed her steps just a bit more. "Well... Good night."

Fabi almost stopped and looked over her shoulder. What were they doing back there? If he was kissing her... Would it really upset her? She missed her dad, but after three years, his memory was getting fainter, and it was getting harder to hear his voice or see his face. Would she mind another man in Mom's life? She wasn't sure. Maybe. Maybe not. At least this was a nice guy, and he loved soccer, so that was a plus in his favor. Finally, she tossed a glance behind her to see her mom stepping back from what appeared to be a quick hug—but had it been more— *had* they been kissing? *Hmm. Okay. Interesting.*

Fabi faced toward the car and took a couple of long strides, not wanting her mom to suspect she'd been listening—or watching. In a matter of seconds, Mom caught up to Fabi and then with Abuela and Sandra a moment later.

Abuela put her hand on her hip and stared at Mom. "So? Did he kiss you?"

Fabi worked hard not to giggle. She'd wanted to ask but didn't dare. Trust Abuela to be blunt and get straight to the point.

Mom gasped. "Soccoro! It's not like that. He wanted

to watch Fabi's soccer game, nothing more. I mean, maybe he did and maybe he didn't, but it's not something I care to talk about—or that I'm going to encourage."

Fabi eyed her mother with a serious look, the kind her mother often gave her when she was going to launch into an inquisition. "Are you sure that's all, Mom?"

Abuela and Sandra laughed, and Fabi dissolved into giggles. Pink rushed into her mother's cheeks but she just shook her head.

ADELA COULDN'T GET David off her mind—and Fabi and Soccoro's teasing after the game—would her daughter be upset if Adela started to have feelings for David. No. That was a stupid thing to even consider. She wasn't staying in San Antonio. There was the European tour and her work in L.A. She mustn't get tangled up in any kind of romantic relationship, no matter how sweet and caring David might be. They piled out of the car and headed for the front steps of Soccoro's home.

Sandra waved and walked to her car parked a few yards up the road. "'Bye, everyone. See you tomorrow."

"Thanks for coming to my game." Fabi waved and headed for the door with Adela and Soccoro on her heels.

They all pulled up short as a man rose from the top step and came to greet them. "Adela? That you?"

Adela halted. "Matias? What in the world are you doing here?"

Matias nodded to Fabi. "Hey there, squirt. Good to see you again. How's the soccer career coming? Ready to start playing in the European leagues yet?"

Adela glared at him. This was not the time or place. "Matias, this is my mother-in-law, Soccoro. Soccoro, my manager, Matias."

Soccoro eyed him for a moment. "Nice to meet you." She turned an inquisitive look on Adela. "Fabi and I are going to fix some snacks. Feel free to invite your manager in when you finish your business." She lifted a hand and then headed for the house right behind a stiff-backed Fabi.

Adela turned to face Matias, but as she did so, she heard the window near the door slide open a tiny bit. Were those two sitting by the window listening? She'd have to be careful what she said to Matias. She crossed her arms. "I can't believe you showed up to the house without calling or asking me for a good time to come."

He threw his hands in the air. "How was I supposed to do that? You aren't answering my calls or apparently listening to my messages."

"Fine. I apologize for that. But you need to quit pressuring me about Europe and the new show. I told you I haven't made a decision yet."

"We're out of time with the network. They need an answer, but you keep putting me off."

Adela sighed. "I love the idea of going to Europe, really I do, Matias. But I'm also struggling with how to make it work. Soccoro needs me here at Romero's, and I love what I'm doing right now—having time for my family—for me. I haven't had that in a long time."

"Seriously, Adela? Are you working at that crumby old diner again? You? The TV star who has her own show and is wanted in Europe? What do you think that's going to do for your career?"

"It is not a crumby old diner!" Anger infused Adela's tone, but she didn't care. He might be her manager, but he had no right to talk that way about something precious to her family—to her.

"You have a chance to make your career with the world's greatest chefs on TV. You would gain international recognition. Why are you squandering your time in a glorified Taco Bell?"

Adela glared at Matias. "That is totally unnecessary. My family comes first. I already explained to you that Fabi doesn't want to go, and I promised her we'd make the decision together."

"Fine. But I need your answer by tomorrow evening. Europe or San Antonio—it's up to you." He swung around, stalked to his car, and then shut his door harder than he needed to. He didn't so much as glance her way before he turned the ignition and headed down the street.

Adela slipped inside the foyer, wondering if Soccoro and Fabi were still crouched by the window. She moved to the living room and found both of them on the couch with the TV going. She smirked and shook her head. "Hey, guys. I'm tired, and I'm going to bed. Thanks for fixing snacks, but I don't feel up to it tonight. Talk to you in the morning."

# Chapter Twenty

SANDRA WALTZED INTO THE COFFEE SHOP and spotted Mya at the same table as last time. "How's your morning going?"

Mya looked up from her phone and grinned. "Well, look who actually showed up *on time*."

"Yeah. Yeah." Truth be told, Sandra had awakened extra early, hoping to escape the house before her grandmother was up and about. Somehow, she'd actually pulled it off. She was still irked with her for the blind date thing, but at least, in the end, Abuela had agreed to talk to the man about cancelling their date. "Let me order. Be right back."

Sandra ordered a large iced coffee and then waited at the other end of the counter for her beverage. She wasn't in the mood for tea today.

"Here you go," the barista said. She must be new because Sandra hadn't seen her before.

"Thanks." Sandra strolled over to Mya and sat.

"How are things?" Mya reached for her medium-sized coffee cup.

Though tempted to dump all her troubles onto her friend, she wouldn't. "I have another date with Victor. Oh, and I went out with Anthony again, but only for ice cream. Short and sweet. No pun intended."

Mya waved her hand. "Hold up. First, that's awesome about Victor, but why would you go out with Anthony when the first date was terrible?"

"It was the means to an end. I'm happy to say, I don't think I'll be hearing from him again." That was a relief too. She didn't need Anthony showing up at Romero's again.

"Girl, I wish my grandma would set me up with someone."

"Trust me. You don't. Can you believe my abuela met some guy at a butcher shop and told him I'd go out with him? She literally set up the date on my behalf, completely breaking the rules of our deal."

Mya's brow furrowed. "I wish I could say I'm surprised, but this sounds like something she'd do. What's your plan?" Mya brought her cup to her lips.

"I told her to deal with it. I wasn't going."

"She actually agreed?" Shock filled Mya's voice.

"I didn't give her the option of disagreeing." For once, she had been firm with her grandmother and told her if the man was hurt it was on her. Though annoyed, Abuela agreed to cancel the date.

"But aren't you a little curious?" Mya asked. "I mean, what if he's the man of your dreams?"

She hadn't considered that, but it didn't matter. "Nope." Until she was fired or someone else took over running Romero's, she had to keep her focus on the diner. Hopefully, Tía Soccoro would see how devoted she was and give her a chance.

Mya crossed her arms and leaned back in her chair.

"I'm very curious. We could go together and check him out from afar."

Sandra nearly spewed iced coffee. "Are you serious?"

"Why not? Why should you get all the men?" Mya raised her chin. "If I like him, I'll ask him out since you're not interested."

Was her friend actually jealous?

"I don't *get* any men," Sandra said. "I've been on a series of disastrous dates. Is that what you want?"

"For a free meal? Why not? And that's not completely accurate. Your date with Victor must have gone well."

"It did." Too well, considering she didn't have the desire to get involved with anyone. That wasn't entirely true. She wanted to see where things went with Victor, but she couldn't get past the fact that he was Romero's competition. "If you really want to meet this man from the butcher shop, I'll find out where my grandma shops and let you know. You can stop in and check him out."

Mya grinned. "Thanks."

Sandra tilted her head. "Why are you suddenly so desperate for a date?" Mya was a beautiful woman but spent her days in the nail salon with mostly women. Maybe meeting men had become difficult since there weren't many who frequented the salon.

"I'm not desperate, but I'm ready to settle down. I'm tired of being single."

"Why am I just now hearing about this? How long have you been on the hunt?"

Mya's face pinked. "A few months. I tried a couple dating apps, but no one there caught my eye. If your grandma approves of this man at the butcher shop, he must be okay. She wouldn't set you up with a loser."

Sandra opened her mouth to say otherwise and then snapped it closed. She might not have cared for the men Abuela set her up with, but they were all good guys with promising careers.

"Why not join me at Victor's team's basketball game? There's sure to be some single men there."

"You mean single dads."

Sandra shrugged. "Probably, but maybe some uncles too."

Mya jogged her head side-to-side. "It could be fun. But I draw the line at being a third wheel on your date."

"Unless someone catches your eye. Then invite him to double with us. That would be fun."

Mya nodded and a slow smile grew on her face. "That's brilliant." She pushed back from the table. "Make sure you text me the name of the butcher shop as well as the time and place of the game."

"Will do." Sandra shouldered her purse and stood while glancing at the time on her phone. "I should get to work. I'm glad we had this talk."

"Me too."

Sandra hugged her friend. "Call if you need anything." Maybe Victor had a single friend for Mya.

SANDRA SPOTTED MYA in the parking lot of the rec center

and waved. She strode toward her. "I'm glad you made it." She hugged her friend.

"Thanks. Me too. The guy at the butcher shop wasn't my type. Not yours either, in case you were wondering."

Sandra grinned. "I wasn't, but I'm not surprised. My grandmother seems to have no clue about the kind of people I like. You look cute tonight."

Mya looked down at her boyfriend style jeans she paired with a white T-shirt and wedge sandals. "Thanks. I figured since it was a sports event, I shouldn't overdo it. You look cute too. I'm surprised you didn't wear a dress."

"I had the same idea as you. Walking up bleachers in a dress didn't sound like a good idea." Her straight leg jeans, sleeveless top, and white sneakers seemed appropriate for the occasion. She'd added a simple gold chain to dress up her look a little. Sandra stopped at the door. "You ready?"

"Ready as I'll ever be. Basketball isn't my favorite."

Sandra nodded. "I know, which is why I deliberately told you a time later than start time so you won't have to sit through all four quarters."

"For real? I hope we made it before half-time."

Mya was definitely on the hunt for a man. Sandra pulled open the rec center's door. The sounds of sneakers squeaking on the gymnasium floor along with a low roar of voices immediately surrounded them. She wrinkled her nose at the smell of old and new sweat that mingled in the air and moved toward a sign that said "Gymnasium."

She pulled open the door and stepped inside. The

stands were to their right. "Looks like there are some open seats in the middle." She led the way along the side of the gym floor and then took the first opening to climb to the seats she'd spied. After climbing past several parents engrossed in the game that was already well into the second quarter, she sank onto the hard metal bench.

Mya jabbed her arm. "There're more people here than I expected."

"Who knew?" She sure hadn't thought the stands would be nearly full. Maybe this game was a bigger deal than Victor had let on.

The referee blew his whistle and then made the traveling motion with his arms.

Mya leaned toward her. "Why's he rolling his arms like that?"

"The kid traveled." Though not a fan of basketball, she understood the basics of the game thanks to high school PE.

"Huh?"

"He isn't supposed to make progress on the court without bouncing the ball in the process." She shot Mya a look of disbelief. They'd attended the same school. Surely, her friend wasn't as clueless as she sounded. Then again, Mya had skipped PE as often as she could get away with.

"Oh." Mya frowned. "The referee is kind of cute. I don't see a ring."

"Don't get your hopes up too much. He might not wear it when he's on the court."

"I didn't think of that."

A tall man with thick, dark hair and a trim physique

sat a few feet from Mya. Sandra didn't see a ring on him either. She elbowed Mya and motioned with her eyes.

The buzzer sounded.

Mya jumped. "What was that for?"

"Half time."

"Oh!" Mya stood. "I didn't see any place to buy refreshments. Did you?"

She shook her head. "I don't think they allow food in the gym." At least that had always been her experience.

Mya frowned. "That makes sense, I guess."

The cute man to their left nodded. "Who are you here to watch play?"

Mya grasped her forearm. "My friend is friends with the coach. I'm here to keep her company."

He nodded at Sandra. "Victor's a good guy. You must be Sandra. He mentioned you'd be here tonight."

Sandra blinked, and her pulse picked up. "He did?" She hadn't expected Victor to mention her to his friends. Then again, why wouldn't he? They were friends after all and worked in the same industry. It stood to reason her name might come up.

"I'm Tate." He walked closer to them.

"It's nice to meet you," Sandra said. "This is my friend Mya."

Mya smiled. "Do you play basketball, Tate."

"I join a pick-up game at a court near my house every Saturday morning."

"Does Victor play too?" Sandra asked. He hadn't mentioned playing, but she had a feeling there was a lot about the man she still needed to learn.

"Sometimes. He's pretty consumed with his food truck. Which is why I had to see the woman who had caught his attention."

Sandra's face heated. "We're just friends. In fact, we're going to grab dessert after the game if you want to join us."

"No, thanks. I don't want to be a third wheel."

"You wouldn't be if Mya comes too, assuming there's not a woman in your life who will mind."

"There isn't." He shrugged. "I'll check with Victor after the game to see if he's cool with us crashing your date." He turned and loped down the bleachers to where the team sat on the side of the gymnasium.

Mya rounded on her. "I can't believe you did that!"

"Why not? I'm your wing woman, like you were mine at the grocery store. Besides, if Victor is friends with him enough to tell him about me and our date, then he must be a good guy."

Mya nodded but still didn't look convinced.

"You're not interested?" She hadn't considered that. "It's only dessert. Not a life commitment."

Mya shrugged. "It's not that. I didn't expect the assist, I guess. You surprised me. He seems like a nice guy."

Tate headed back up the bleaches, wearing a grin. "We're good."

"Cool," Mya said.

The teams moved back onto the court.

"See you after." Tate sat and focused on the game.

Mya pulled Sandra down beside her. "I so owe you."

"Don't thank me yet. You have no idea how he eats. He might chew with his mouth open."

Mya's jaw opened. "No way."

"Trust me. I've seen it all at Romero's. Things no one should have to witness."

Mya giggled.

"What's so funny?" Sandra kept her focus on Victor who stood on the side line clapping his hands and hollering out to his team.

"I'm imagining a room full of people eating like animals."

She jerked her head toward Mya.

Mya pretended to eat straight from an imaginary bowl. She looked at Sandra with puppy dog eyes.

Sandra laughed. "Maybe you should moonlight as a writer. You have quite an imagination."

"Really?" Mya shook her head. "I don't think writing is for me. I've never been good at it." School had never been Mya's thing period. She much preferred to be creative, which is why she went to school to learn to do nails and makeup. She learned to do hair too but claimed she was awful at it. Sandra had never volunteered to let Mya practice on her, so she didn't have a clue if her friend truly was bad or not.

Other than cheering when Victor's team made a basket, they watched the game in silence after that. It'd been a long day and it seemed they both needed a little down time. Sandra jumped when a sudden roar filled the gymnasium. She glanced toward Tate who leapt to his feet and did a fist pump.

Mya slid closer to her. "You think the game is over?"

"Yes, and if Tate's response is any indication, Victor's team won." She'd spaced out for the last bit of the game and had lost track of the score even though it was on the electric board high on the wall.

A surge of people headed for the exit.

"Should we wait in the lobby for Victor?" Mya motioned toward the doors.

Sandra focused on Victor as he huddled with his team. "You and Tate can if you want, but I'm going to wait here. The lobby is packed."

Tate stepped down to the level in front of them. "What a game! Did you see that buzzer beater at the end?" His smile filled his face.

Mya nodded. "It was something. I couldn't believe that kid launched the ball from the middle of the court and made it in."

How had she missed that? Sandra couldn't even say where her mind had gone. It had been a long day for sure.

The team dispersed, and Victor turned to face them, all smiles. Clearly, he was basking in his team's big win. "Everyone ready? I thought we could go to Crepeccino."

Mya held her hand to her heart. "I *love* that place. Have you been, Sandra?"

"Never." She'd heard of it though. It was considered one of the top places in the city for dessert.

"Should we all ride together?" Tate asked. "My SUV will hold all of us comfortably."

Sandra watched for Victor's reaction. If they all rode together, they wouldn't have any alone time. Then again, they were friends. This wasn't a real date.

Victor nodded. "Good idea. Let's go. I'm in the mood to celebrate."

About twenty minutes later, they strolled into Crepeccino. Several people were in line, and many of the tables were taken. Sandra breathed in the scent of chocolate, coffee, and waffles. Her stomach rumbled. "What a fun shop. I love the colors. Turquoise and brown are one of my favorite color combos." From the shiny chocolate-colored tile floors to the swirly feature light over the dining area, this place spoke of class and fun at the same time. "Oh look, they have gelato."

Mya chuckled. "You sound like a kid in a candy store."

They moved to the line and stood as couples.

"You know gelato's my favorite." If the ice cream store around the corner from Romero's had gelato, she'd be at least ten pounds heavier.

Victor caught her gaze. "Mine too. What's your favorite flavor."

Her face heated. She didn't want to admit she loved vanilla gelato, especially after giving Anthony such a hard time about the flavor, but thankfully, Victor didn't know what she'd said.

A slow smile grew on his face. "Now I have to know."

"There's not a flavor I don't like, but vanilla gelato is amazing."

His eyes twinkled. "Then vanilla you shall have."

They ordered, paid, and then waited for their gelato. Victor handed her bowl to her. "For the lady." He reached for his bowl—a triple scoop of strawberry, chocolate, and vanilla.

Gelato envy made Sandra's mouth water. She should have gotten what he'd ordered. She shrugged away the thought. Her double scoop of vanilla would be delicious. They settled at a table for four in the middle of the seating area, a couple on each side. Not the romantic setting they'd had on their last date, but this was still fun.

Victor glanced toward Tate and Mya and leaned in close to her ear. "How'd that happen?"

"He introduced himself during half-time as your friend," Sandra spoke softly. "He knew who I was, so I asked if he wanted to join us."

A twinkle filled his eyes. "Playing matchmaker?"

"Maybe." She scooped a bite of gelato into her mouth and closed her eyes, focusing on the burst of vanilla. "How'd you find this place?" She'd never noticed it in the strip mall before.

"Someone told me about it."

Mya sat across from her, and Tate sat across from Victor and each held milkshakes.

If Sandra didn't love gelato so much, she would have ordered a shake too. She shifted and looked at Victor. "I know the pros have a much longer season, but does your win tonight end your season?"

Victor nodded. "I'm going to miss it."

Tate clapped him on the shoulder. "Look at the bright side. Now you have more time to spend socializing."

Victor raised a brow. "There is that." His gaze rested on Sandra.

Sandra's face warmed, and she quickly shoveled another bite into her mouth.

Mya placed her milkshake on the table. "What do you do, Tate?"

Tate hesitated and dipped his chin. "I teach high school math."

Mya shuddered playfully. "You realize that's a four-letter word?"

Tate frowned. "And that's why I hate telling people what I do. It's always the same reaction."

"I'm sorry. I didn't mean to make you feel bad," Mya said. "Math was my worst subject. I almost didn't graduate because of Algebra II. That class was a nightmare."

"Yeah. That particular one gives our students a hard time too. I teach geometry and calculus."

Sandra scooped another bite into her mouth, more than willing to let the other couple carry the conversation.

"What about you, Mya?" Tate asked. "What do you do?"

"I'm a nail technician."

"You're a creative. Cool."

Mya sat a bit taller and beamed. "You should stop in sometime and get a manicure. Mani's aren't only for women."

"Do you have a lot of male clients?"

She shook her head. "Not really, but men are coming in more now than they did even a couple of years ago."

"Interesting. I'll think about it." Tate raised his straw to his lips and took a long draw.

Sandra liked this guy, and she could tell her friend did too. She almost motioned with her head and eyes to Victor that they should leave and then remembered they'd all ridden here together.

Victor laughed. "I'm sorry, but I can't imagine you letting anyone do your nails."

Mya frowned. "He doesn't need to have them polished. Having well-manicured hands are a sign of class." She looked pointedly at Victor's short nails. "You do those yourself?"

He nodded.

This conversation was tanking the mood. Sandra needed to do something fast. "So, Victor, I'd love to hear how you got into cooking." They'd covered a lot of topics on their last date, but cooking hadn't been one of them.

"I took a cooking class on a dare and discovered I really liked the culinary arts. The rest is history."

Sandra breathed a little easier with their conversation on safe ground now.

Tate raised his phone which displayed the time. "I hate to say it, but I need to take everyone back to the gym."

"No problem." Victor stood and bussed their table.

This guy was gold. Sandra liked him more every time they were together. She reminded herself he was the competition, and she couldn't fall for him. Though it might be too late.

# Chapter Twenty-One

ADELA STEERED INTO THE PARKING LOT behind Romero's and braked to a stop. She understood why the atmosphere had been strained after the conversation two nights ago with Matias. She'd bought herself another day with him by texting and telling him she was seriously considering it but needed more time to talk Fabi into it. However, when she'd tried to broach the subject with Fabi yesterday, her daughter had simply huffed and shut herself in her room. She sat behind the wheel and didn't move as Soccoro and Fabi both climbed out.

Fabi shut the door and took a step away but paused. She slowly turned and opened her door and peeked in. "Mom? You coming?"

"Yeah, sweetie. Sorry. Just thinking."

Fabi scowled. "I know what about, and I don't want to go to Europe."

Adela pushed out of the car and followed her stomping daughter's footsteps into Romero's, still clueless what she planned to do. She couldn't make Fabi, Soccoro, and Matias all happy, not to mention herself. And she wasn't even certain what she wanted for herself. An image of David's face flitted across her mind followed by one of European grandeur. She sighed. She hated making decisions, and there was certainly no guarantee David would ever be more than a friend—or that Fabi would ever agree to Europe. Sometimes parenting—and being an adult—was hard.

Soccoro had been walking slowly to the door, and Fabi reached it at the same time Soccoro gripped the knob to swing it open.

Adela increased her speed. "Hey? Guys?"

They both swung around, guarded expressions on both faces.

"I think we need to have a family meeting after work. That okay?"

Fabi crossed her arms over her chest. "You made a decision, didn't you? You decided to go to Europe and already told that old manager."

"I told you, I'm not making that big of a decision without you, but I want all three of us to discuss it. Can you do that?" She tried to encourage both of them with a smile, but Soccoro's face remained impassive, and Fabi appeared near tears.

A few minutes later, Fabi was washing dishes, and Adela worked with the prep cook to ready the kitchen for the upcoming lunch rush.

Sandra walked in and stopped next to Soccoro. "Do you have a minute?"

"Sure. What's up?" Soccoro turned and met Sandra's gaze.

"You need to review these applications and resumes. I've posted ads online and in the window since Manny quit. I've reviewed all the applications and put together my shortlist." She held out the paperwork.

Soccoro placed one hand on her hip but didn't take the papers. "Adela might stay and cook. We don't need to rush to fill the position yet."

Sandra huffed and cast a glance at Adela. "I can't imagine she's going to want to give up her TV show to work in our kitchen for long."

Adela arched her brows but didn't reply. She hadn't decided what she wanted to do, but giving up her show and staying here long term had never truly seemed an option. What was Soccoro doing talking that way when she knew she hadn't made up her mind?

Soccoro lifted her chin an inch. "You don't know that for sure. This is a decision I need to make."

Sandra thrust the papers into Soccoro's hands. "Neither do you. And as the assistant manager, I'm asking that you at least review these applications."

"All right, all right." Soccoro took them but shook her head as she watched Sandra head back to the dining room.

SOCCORO SCANNED THE applications and resumes. She didn't see a single one that jumped out at her. Each one seemed flat. Boring. Without promise. Dare she hope that Adela might stay? She felt like a woman who had sunk into quicksand, and instead of flopping onto her back to keep from sinking, she was stabbing her feet deeper into the muck.

A tap at the door to the kitchen made her turn around. Patrick stood in the doorway grinning at her. She placed the resumes on a sideboard and walked over to crack open the door. "We don't open until eleven, Patrick."

His quiet laugh almost made Soccoro smile. "I wanted one of those pork belly tamales for breakfast, but I knew you wouldn't be open yet. I thought I'd beat the lunch rush. I haven't been able to stop thinking about the excellent food here."

Soccoro shook her head and tried not to frown. Right now, the last thing she wanted to deal with was a customer, even if it was a handsome one like Patrick. "*Lo siento, amigo.* No can do. But it's only a short time until we start serving. Maybe your stomach can hold out a little longer?"

Patrick took a step forward, blocking the door. "What's wrong? You don't seem like your chipper, smiling self today. Everything okay?"

She shook her head, wanting nothing more than to go to her office and bury her head. Nothing seemed right in her world right now. "Nothing. I'm fine." But the words sounded flat, even to her own ears.

"Fine? You don't look fine to me. Want to take a quick walk? It's a beautiful day and not hot yet. Maybe a stroll will help put whatever is bothering you into perspective?" He motioned toward the exit and gave her a tentative smile.

Soccoro hesitated for only a second and then gave a decisive nod. Maybe an impartial listener was exactly what she needed. "Sí. Gracias. That sounds like a very good plan." She swung toward the kitchen. "Adela? I'm going to take a quick walk with Patrick before the rush starts. You'll be okay?"

Adela looked up from her prep work. "Of course. Good idea. Enjoy." She waved her hand toward the door and then returned to concentrating on the table of colorful foods in front of her.

Soccoro eased the door shut behind her and then stepped out into the humid air. She'd seen cooler temps in San Antonio, but at least the heat hadn't hit its peak yet. She fanned her face. Maybe it was her age as well. She chuckled and then turned her attention to Patrick. "It feels good to get outside. Gracias." She fell into step beside him, wondering how much she should share with this kind-hearted man who had been a good friend over the years.

He nudged her arm. "So? I can tell something has been on your mind. Is it still the worry over your business that's bothering you?"

She slowed her pace. "Sí. I'm trying to decide what's best for me to do with Romero's. Having Adela and Fabi here have been wonderful—almost like returning to the old days when Mauricio was alive. But Adela has an offer to do a new TV show while traveling in Europe cooking with the world's greatest chefs. How can Romero's or San Antonio compete with that?"

"Maybe you don't try to compete." He reached out and took her hand and gave it a gentle squeeze. "Maybe you only need to listen to her heart—to be supportive and help her find what is best for her and her daughter. All the rest will fall into place."

She squeezed his hand in return and then pulled hers away, not wanting to give him the wrong impression—although she had to admit, the warmth of his touch had been pleasant. "I want to be supportive, really I do. But what if that's not what she wants to do? I mean, I'm not sure that her heart is in traveling to Europe. She belongs here in San Antonio, and so does Fabi."

Patrick raised a brow and gave her a small smile. "Are you sure it's not her heart but yours that feels that way?"

She shrugged. "Ever since my son died, she's been running—either to something else or away from the memories. I think it hurts her too much to be here without Mauricio, but I know he'd want her to be with us. With family, not traipsing around the world making her daughter unhappy."

"I'm sorry, Soccoro." He drew to a stop and faced her and then put his hands on her upper arms. "I know how much you care about her, but sometimes you have to let your kids figure things out on their own. Trust me. I know how hard that can be. I wanted to lay everything out for my son at my business, but he has a good head and is making wise decisions. I have a good feeling about Adela. I think you can trust her to do what's right for herself and your granddaughter."

She reached up and stroked his cheek and then took a step back, warmth flooding her face. "Thank you, Patrick. That's good advice. Gracias."

"Of course." He tipped his head.

She gave him a saucy grin. "You still want that pork

belly tamale? We're opening in a few minutes. I know Adela would be happy to make you one before the rush hits."

"Well..." Patrick dropped his head for a moment, met her gaze, and took a deep breath. "I didn't only come for a tamale, although it does sound wonderful. Remember what we discussed the other day, about maybe getting together sometime outside of Romero's? I was wondering if you'd care to come to dinner with me soon. My treat, wherever you'd like to go."

Her heart gave a little jolt and then settled into a steady rhythm. Maybe Romero's and her family weren't the only things that mattered in her life.

THE OUTSIDE KITCHEN door opened and closed softly. Adela laid down her knife and turned to smile at her mother-in-law. "Did you have a nice walk?" Her brows rose at the high color in Soccoro's cheeks and the unusual sparkle in her eyes. "I can see you did."

Soccoro shook her finger but grinned. "Never you mind. If you're done prepping, could I talk to you for a few minutes in my office?"

"I'm not quite finished. Can it wait?"

"Maybe your prep cook can finish? It will only take a moment, por favor?"

"Okay, be right there." She nodded to the prep cook and gave a finger wave to Fabi standing by the dishwashing station. "Back in a minute."

She slid into the seat across from the desk in

Soccoro's cramped office and looked around. This was another space that still needed renovating, but some of the family and business photos on the walls made her smile. She turned to Soccoro who smiled as she followed Adela's gaze around the wall of memories.

"Que pasa?" Adela leaned forward, not wanting to rush but feeling the need to get back to her station.

Soccoro waited a moment and then blurted out words fast, as though she'd stored them up for way too long. "How would you like to take over the running of Romero's? Not just as the cook, but to have complete oversight. Permanently." She sat back against her chair as though the sentences had taken all the strength she had to get them out.

"Excuse me?" Adela wasn't certain she'd heard her right. "Take over?"

"Sí. I can't run this place forever, and I don't want to sell it. I want you to have it. That's what Mauricio would want as well."

Adela let her breath out in a whoosh. "Wow. I'm honored. Truly I am. Thank you. But I don't know what to say to such a generous offer. I have my career to think about too."

"I know it's not a decision you can make right now. Take a little time to think about it, but I wanted to ask you before you give your manager an answer about Europe. It's up to you what you decide, but you're the only person I'd completely trust with Romero's."

"What about Sandra?" Adela shook her head, still unsure that she was following. "She's learning the business and working hard to make it succeed."

"I know, but I don't feel Sandra is ready for that kind of responsibility. She might never be. You'll at least think about it?"

The door that hadn't completely closed behind Adela burst open, and Sandra stood in the entrance, her eyes flashing with anger. "I can't believe this! I was walking by and heard my name, so I stopped. And what do I hear? You're offering to give Romero's to Adela and cut me out. After a week? After all I've done to help you?"

Soccoro held up her hand. "Wait, Sandra. I'm not cutting you out. But Adela worked here for close to ten years. She's older and has more experience. There would still be a place for you here."

"Ha! As what, a prep cook or waitress? She's never run a business. She cooks on a TV show." She planted her fists on her hips and glared, but Adela clearly saw hurt shining from her eyes.

"Hold it." Adela pushed to her feet. "I didn't say I want to take over Romero's."

"Why?" Sandra sniffed. "My dream job isn't good enough for you?"

"Wait!" Soccoro shook her head. "Where is all this coming from, Sandra?"

Sandra spun from Adela to Soccoro. "I know you feel like Adela walks on water and can do no wrong, and I'm just your lowly assistant manager, since you're clearly talking management status here. I mean, I know you're the owner and everything, but I think you're making a big mistake." She sniffed again and swiped at her nose. "The only reason Adela is helping us is she feels guilty for leaving when she did. Deep down, she knows, and I think you do too, that she's going to leave again. Even if she agrees to take over, it won't last forever, and you'll be without any managers by then."

"Hey!" Adela took a step closer to Sandra. "You can't know that. You're tossing things out that you have no way of knowing."

"Yeah, just keep telling yourself that. I'm done. I'm going for a walk. I need to get out of here." Sandra tore off her apron and tossed it on the floor. Then she pivoted and stormed out the door.

Soccoro stared wide-eyed at Adela for a moment and then raced after Sandra. "Wait! We need to talk."

Adela picked up the apron and carefully hung it on a hook behind the door. Her gaze fell on a newspaper clipping tacked to the wall. "Local Cook Leaves Hot Grill for Hollywood." Adela bit her lip. Could Sandra be right? If she did stay, would the lure of Hollywood or another European tour lure her away again? Was it fair even agreeing to think about Soccoro's offer?

# Chapter Twenty-Two

SANDRA STOOD OUTSIDE ROMERO'S GULPING FRESH air. Tía Soccoro's words replayed in her mind. How could her aunt say she didn't think Sandra would ever be ready to take over Romero's? Maybe Anthony was right. Her job didn't matter to anyone but her. Apparently, her education was for nothing too if her own aunt didn't believe in her.

She swallowed the lump in her throat and walked away from Romero's. A tear trickled down her cheek. She swiped it away. Before she even realized what she was doing, she was standing at Victor's food truck.

"*Hola!*" Victor said from the window. "This is a surprise." He frowned. "What's wrong?"

She raised a shoulder and shook her head.

He said something to someone in the truck, and the next thing she knew Victor guided her to a nearby table. He sat across from her. "Did someone die?"

"No. Only my dream." Her gaze met his. "My aunt doesn't believe in me. I thought…" She sucked in a breath. She shouldn't be dumping all of this on Victor. He didn't need her drama. "I'm sorry. I don't know why I'm telling you this." She started to rise, but Victor's hand on hers stopped her.

"Stay."

"What about the lunch rush?"

"Look around. No one here. They're all at Romero's. I was about to send my help home. Now, what's wrong?"

She glanced toward the truck and then scanned the area around them. He was right. Foot traffic was sparse at best. She took a breath and let it out slowly. "I put my heart and soul into Romero's. Adela didn't. She left for Hollywood, found fame, and is unbelievably successful. If I had half the success she did, we wouldn't be talking right now. It's not fair."

"*Mi madre* used to tell me all the time 'Life is not fair, *hijo*. What you do with what you are dealt is up to you.'" He looked tenderly into Sandra's eyes.

"But my aunt doesn't believe in me. She has stars in her eyes. Adela is the only one she thinks can save Romero's. I'm so sick of Adela. She is so stinking perfect! Everyone loves her. Even the reporter who annihilated her in an interview has fallen for her." She winced when her tirade at Romero's replayed in her mind. She placed her elbows on the table and rested her head in her hands.

She'd spoken out of turn and had no business talking like that to her aunt and Adela. Her stomach knotted tighter as the full scope of what she'd said hit her. What had she done? "I said things I shouldn't have. I was awful."

"I'm sure you weren't that bad." Victor rubbed her arm gently.

She looked up and met his tender gaze. "No. I lost my temper. It wasn't pretty." If only she could reverse

MIRALEE FERRELL and KIMBERLY ROSE JOHNSON

time and take a breath before she let her temper get the best of her.

Victor gently touched her hands. "No one is perfect. That includes Adela."

"I know. Thanks for saying that, but I really wish time would go in reverse. But what do I do?"

"Seems to me, you are at a crossroads and need to make a decision. Humble yourself and go back to Romero's to apologize or walk away."

Her stomach knotted tighter. "Those are my only two options?" She expected him to tell her everything would be okay. That things would blow over, and that she was justified for getting angry but needed to think before exploding at the mouth. Could she go back? She buried her face in her hands.

"You owe your family an apology," Victor said gently. "Even if you choose to move on from Romero's."

She lowered her hands and met his gaze. "Sí. You're right. I do need to apologize. It's too late to take back my words. I'm afraid the damage is done. Even with an apology, it won't change that I hurt my family. It's too late for me at Romero's. My dream of running the diner is over."

"Maybe. Maybe not. It seems to me, what's more important is your family. Do you want to restore your relationship with them or walk away and do life on your own?"

She gasped. Was it really that serious? Sandra ducked her chin and swallowed the lump in her throat. "I know what I need to do, but it's not going to be easy."

"Doing the right thing is often the hard thing. I'll be praying for you." He stood and offered his hand.

She placed hers in his and stood. "Thanks."

"Let me know how it goes?" He raised a brow.

"I will. Thanks for praying. I need all the help I can get."

Victor opened his arms, and she stepped into them. "You've got this. Be courageous and strong."

"Thank you."

He lowered his arms.

She immediately missed his touch. "Okay. Here it goes." She strode toward Romero's, guilt weighing down her every step. *Lord, please help me.*

# Chapter Twenty-Three

DAVID STROLLED INTO ROMERO'S, AND HIS heart rate accelerated. He'd decided it was time to put his plan into action. When Adela attended his book signing and invited him to Fabi's game, it had given him hope that there might be more in store for them. And that kiss—well—the kiss that got shortened way faster than he'd wanted to when Adela had pulled away. He figured it had to be because she was nervous with her family only a few yards ahead of them, but a little doubt still niggled, making him not as sure of himself as he'd like to be.

Through the window in the kitchen, he glimpsed Adela placing a plate on the window opening for the server to take to a customer. It smelled great—but was that a frown pulling at Adela's pretty lips? She appeared tense—but maybe it had simply been a stressful day. Hopefully, he could make it a little better and lighten the mood. He strode forward until he stood in the doorway to the kitchen. "Well, if it's not the best tamale maker in town...and the best looking one as well." He grinned at her, but she dumped more salsa on the dish she was creating and gritted her teeth. *Oops.* That hadn't been the reaction he'd been hoping for.

Over at the dishwashing station, Fabi lifted a hand

dripping with suds. "Hey, David! How's it going?" She beckoned at him, sending soap bubbles flying. "Come on in. We don't let customers come in, but you're special." She giggled.

He grinned at her, walked into the kitchen, and stood close to Adela. "Thanks."

She didn't so much as raise her eyes from what she was doing. "Sorry. We're busy. I don't have time to talk."

"I promise I'm not trying to cut in line or get you to serve me first." He winked at Fabi.

She giggled again. "I think Mom would be okay with that."

Soccoro dinged the bell at the window. "I need an order of *nachos de chicharron rápido*."

Adela waved her hand. "Got it." She brushed a strand of hair off her forehead with the back of her hand and groaned. "Ugh. How did that slip out?"

David glanced over at Fabi whose smile had turned to a frown. He lowered his voice and stepped a half-pace closer to Adela. "I'll make this fast as I can see you're busy. Would you be free for dinner tomorrow night? I thought it might be fun to check out my friend Bart's restaurant, that Peruvian place. He's got a couple of new dishes on the menu I think you'd enjoy. I've only tried one, and it was excellent."

She glanced up only long enough to barely meet his eyes and then returned her attention to the dish she was working on. "Yeah—David—I don't know."

He started and blinked. What, no Davey? It was David now? Something definitely had her flustered—or upset. He watched as she seemed to lose her concentration and hesitated as she put the nacho dish together, and he took a step back. "Hey, this was bad timing on my part. How about we talk about it later when you're not so busy?"

This time she didn't look up at all. "No. I mean, I don't know if I'll be around tomorrow at all." She took a deep breath and faced him. "It's been a fun week, but I don't think I belong at Romero's anymore."

"Okay—I'm not sure I get what you're saying. I think you fit perfectly here. It's almost like you never left."

She winced, and he bit his lip. Apparently, the wrong thing to say.

She shook her head. "You don't really know me beyond a couple of interviews and hanging out together once or twice."

"Yeah." He stuffed his hands into the back of his jeans' pockets. "And I'm trying to change that right now by inviting you out to dinner tomorrow." He hadn't realized he'd started talking louder until he saw Fabi's wide eyes and small smile. Could Adela's daughter be rooting for him? His heart warmed at the thought. She was such a great kid. He'd love to be involved more in her life, as well.

"My manager is pushing me to host a summer cooking series in Europe. Cooking with Monica Galetti and Mossimo Bottura would be a dream come true for me and do amazing things for my career. And here I am breaking my back and killing my feet standing over a hot grill in the summer in San Antonio. I've come too far to start from scratch again."

David tipped his head to one side. "I thought Romero's was important to you."

"It is important, but that doesn't mean I have to work here for the rest of my life."

"What's really going on, Adela? Talk to me. This is Davey, remember?" He tried to grin at her but it fell short.

She kept her head down, refusing to meet his eyes. "The interview is over, David. I need to get my work done."

He jerked back his head and widened his eyes, feeling as though she'd slapped him. "Bueno. If you say so." He gave a small salute to Fabi. "Have a great day, kiddo." It seemed there was nothing more to say to Adela, so he spun around and walked out the door, and apparently, out of her life.

FABI STARED AT her mother and then looked pointedly at the door where David had disappeared. She had a feeling he was gone forever. Mom had really hurt him with the way she'd acted. It was rare for her to ever see her mother cold or rude to anyone, but she'd hit him hard with her attitude.

Mom stepped over to the window, placed the plate of nachos there, and then dinged the bell. "Order up." When she turned back around, Fabi saw her wipe her cheek with the back of her hand. Had that been a tear she saw before Mom swiped it away? If she was sad, why had she sent David away? None of it made sense.

Over an hour later, her grandmother wiped down

the counter and turned to Fabi. "Great job keeping up with all the dishes and cleanup, baby. You're really fast. I might have to hire you permanently." She put her hand at the base of her back. "I'm not as young as I used to be. We haven't had a crowd like this since the good old days. I can't believe Sandra wasn't here to help."

Mom came out of the kitchen and beckoned to Fabi. "Yeah. I need to talk to you about the good old days."

Her grandmother nodded. "Sure, mija."

"You too, Fabi. It's time for another family meeting."

Fabi almost felt sick to her stomach. She knew that tone. It wasn't going to be happy news, and she'd almost bet Mom had decided to go to Europe after all. She dragged her feet but managed to make it to the open kitchen door leading into the dining area. Mom and Abuela stood on each side of a small table, but neither of them sat.

Mom closed her eyes for a long moment, opened them slowly, and focused on Abuela. "I've thought about your offer, and I can't accept it. Romero's is my past, not my future." She took off her apron and draped it over the back of the chair pushed under the table. "I'm taking the job in Europe and leaving San Antonio."

"What?" Her grandmother looked like Fabi felt, as though she'd hit the water in a pool in a belly flop and all the air got knocked out.

"Mom! No. You said you wouldn't make this decision without me. I'm not going, and you can't make me." Tears formed in her eyes and threatened to race down her face, but she wiped them away.

"I can't stay here. Sandra was right. I came back because I felt guilty for leaving. I'm the one who took Mauricio away from the home and job that he loved, so I could have my own cooking show. I don't deserve for you to give me Romero's." She looked from Fabi to Grandmother, and her eyes seemed almost lifeless.

Fabi was too hurt right now to care. She crossed her arms over her chest. "You promised me. I want to stay here. I'm not going to Europe."

"I know, and I don't want to ruin your summer. I'm guessing your grandmother would let you stay with her while I'm away. I'll be home by the time school starts, and we'll go back to California together. Does that work for both of you?"

Fabi didn't wait for her grandmother to answer. This was not how things were supposed to be. Mom was supposed to fall for David so she'd want to stay here at Romero's. "But this is home, Mom. Not L.A. I love it here. Why can't we stay here forever?" Now she couldn't wipe the tears away as they were coming too fast to keep up with.

Her grandmother reached out and drew Fabi into a hug. "You know I'd love to have Fabi here, but you should be the one looking after your daughter, Adela, not me."

Her mother simply shook her head and turned away.

"I hope you'll change your mind, mija."

Mom's voice was so soft Fabi barely heard her. "I won't."

Fabi broke out of Abuela's embrace. "You can't do this, Mom. I don't want you to go. You need to stay here with us."

Mom finally looked up and met Fabi's gaze, and her eyes were filled with tears as well. "I have to, Fabi. Someday you'll understand why." She held out her arms, and Fabi hesitated for only a moment. She stepped into them and hugged her mom as hard as she could.

"I need to talk to Matias so he can make arrangements with the network and book a flight." She walked over and hugged Abuela and then headed to the kitchen. "I'll get my purse and make a phone call."

Abuela bit her lip. "Sí. Adios, *mi hija.*"

Mom turned around and gave them one more long look. "I love you both." As she headed out the door, Sandra came in. Mom gave Sandra a strange look. "Good luck, Sandra."

Soccoro FELT AS though the ground had opened up and was ready to close after her. She'd had no idea that Adela had felt so strongly or that she'd felt so much guilt about taking Mauricio away from San Antonio years ago. But that was so far in the past. Why did it matter now?

Sandra cocked her head. "Where's she going?"

Soccoro narrowed her eyes. How much should she say? And would it change anything now? Sandra was her niece, and Soccoro understood why she'd been hurt at what she'd overheard earlier, but she'd also said some cutting things to Adela. "She's going to Europe. As soon as her agent can book a flight."

Sandra seemed first to brighten and then her face

sobered. "Really?"

Fabi burst out crying, and Soccoro turned to hug her. Time to deal with Sandra later. This little girl needed her now.

Sandra moved up and patted Fabi's shoulder. "What's wrong, honey? Is she making you go with her?"

That was all Soccoro could take. Sandra needed a wake-up call, and she was going to give it to her. "What's wrong is that her mother is leaving because of your jealousy. If you hadn't said all those hurtful things earlier, this wouldn't be happening."

Sandra's mouth sagged open. Then she snapped it shut and stiffened. "You always side with Adela. Never with me. And I'm your niece. She's your daughter-in-law."

Fabi pulled away from Sandra and Soccoro and faced Sandra. She stomped her foot. "My mom has always been nice to you. Always. She's never said a mean thing or done anything bad to you. She came back here to try to help Abuela—to try to help save Romero's. Why did you say mean things to her?"

Sandra bit her lip and looked away for a moment. Then she faced them both. "I didn't feel like we needed a TV chef fixing our problems." She swung toward Soccoro. "But you wouldn't listen to me. You don't think I have anything worthwhile to share or that I'm any real value to the business. I shouldn't have said the things I did, and I'm very sorry, but it's really hard, Tía Soccoro, to know you don't think I'll ever be able to run this place. After all the work I've done here."

Soccoro gave a slow nod. "I can see why you'd feel that way, but I did listen. I invested in renovations that I couldn't really afford because you felt strongly that we needed them. And yes, they did help. A lot." She drew in a shallow breath. "I'm sorry if you feel I've taken you for granted—if you felt you didn't have value in my eyes. That's not the case at all. You are still young, and you have much to learn, but you've done a good job for me, and I do appreciate you."

"Thank you. That means a lot." Sandra's voice caught, and she seemed to wilt. "I'm so sorry," she whispered the words. "More sorry than I can say. For what I said to Adela and how I've acted all this time. I don't know what to do to make it right."

Fabi spun around and marched for the exit.

Soccoro held out her hand to stop her, but she was too late. Fabi opened the door. "Fabi? Wait. *Donde vos.*"

"Where am I going? Where do you think?" She shot a hard look at Sandra. "To get my mom back."

Sandra and Soccoro rushed after Fabi as she raced to the door and then stood scanning the area outside. Had Adela called Matias, and he'd come to pick her up?

Sandra slowed next to Fabi. "I'm so sorry, Fabi. I shouldn't have opened my big mouth and said the things I did."

Fabi shook her off. "Sorry won't help now. Besides, you didn't apologize to my mom. That's who needs to hear it, not me."

"I agree. But it can't hurt to try. Are you with me?"

Fabi stared at her and then gave a slow nod and a

little smile. "Absolutely. We'll be back, Abuela. Hopefully with Mom. I'm pretty sure I know where she'd stop before she leaves town. Pray that she listens!"

Soccoro stood there stunned. "But who will run the counter and cook and wash dishes?" She threw her hands in the air. "Never mind. *Váyanse!* It's quiet now anyway. Go! God and I will figure it out."

The door swung open, and Sandra and Fabi rushed out past Patrick.

Soccoro grinned and grabbed his hand. "Patrick! An answer to prayer. You know how to wash dishes?"

# Chapter Twenty-Four

ADELA SAT STARING OUT THE WINDOW as Matias expertly wove through the traffic on the way to the airport. They'd made a quick stop at Soccoro's house so she could pack, but he'd assured her she'd find most of the things she needed when she landed in Paris. Her heart was screaming at her to go back to Romero's—to give her daughter one more hug and apologize to Soccoro for leaving her without notice, but she knew if she did, she'd never get on that plane. And right now, she knew that was the best thing for everyone.

Matias slowed and then stopped for a red light. "I'm so glad you finally came to your senses and decided to go on this tour." He gave her a big smile.

She tried to return it, but it fell flat. "Yeah. Me too."

"You don't sound like it. Why the long face? Something happen that I should know about?"

She shrugged but didn't manage to muster a reply.

Her heart quaked remembering the hopeful look in David's eyes when he'd asked her to dinner—and the pain that took its place when she made it clear she wasn't interested. The problem was, she was far too interested for her own good—or for his. She didn't know what she wanted anymore, but it definitely wasn't to leave her family or the man she was coming to care for, to fly off to work with chefs she'd never met and didn't care if she ever did meet. Europe wasn't home.

"Hey! You're going to be an international cooking star, right up there with Jamie Oliver. This is what you've always wanted, right?"

"Sure. Yeah. I suppose I have." She turned her head to look out the window. The last thing she wanted right now was to discuss this with Matias. The car moved on and she saw Tacos Rápidos up ahead. Adela didn't think her heart could sink much lower.

She turned to face him. "Do you mind if we make a quick stop?"

"What? Why? You can't be late for your flight."

"Seriously. Please pull over."

He slowed and stopped at the curb only a half block from the taco stand.

"One second. I won't be long." She stepped out onto the curb and glanced back to see him checking his phone.

There was only one person at the order window, so this shouldn't take long. It was going to be a long flight, but there was no better place to grab a meal before she left than here. She was about to step up to the window when she heard a car door slam and feet slapping the sidewalk in a run. The man at the window beckoned her forward. "What can I get you?"

"Gracias. *Tres lengua tacos y una agua fresca de sandia.*"

"Adela!" At the sound of a familiar voice, Adela swung around and faced Sandra with a breathless Fabi on her heels.

"Sandra. Fabi! What in the world are you doing here? And how did you know where I'd be?" She placed a hand over her hammering heart.

Fabi bounced on her toes. "You always stop at Tacos Rápidos. It was Dad's favorite place to eat besides Romero's. He always stopped here as soon as we got to town, and it was the last place we'd eat before we left town. I kind of thought you might remember that and make Matias stop."

Sandra reached out her hand but let her arm drop. "I'm so sorry, Adela. I was horrible and so wrong in what I said to you."

Adela shook her head. "No. It was all true. I did come back here because I felt guilty for leaving. It's been hard being here without Mauricio. I feel like I had a part in his dying." She struggled to keep in the tears that once again threatened to overwhelm her.

"Mom! That's not true at all. Dad died because he had a heart attack and then wrecked the car. The doctors said so. You had nothing to do with that. I can't believe you'd blame yourself for that."

"I know, baby. You're right. But he should have been here, surrounded by his family, not off in L.A. to make me happy. That was incredibly selfish of me."

"No, Mom. It wasn't your fault. Dad told me how proud he was of you—of your career and how hard you worked. He was never upset about moving."

Sandra reached out again and touched Adela's arm, and Adela froze, not sure what to think. "Fabi's right, Adela. You can't blame yourself for following your heart and doing what you loved. You need to know that I said those things to you because I was jealous, not because any of them were true. You're a famous chef, something I will never be. But that wasn't why. It was because you belong at Romero's. You did what I always wanted to do but never could—you turned the business around and made people want to come—and all in a week or so. I've never done that. I don't like to admit that, but it's true, and I'm so sorry for how I've been treating you since you arrived."

Adela nodded and then looked at the car when the blast of a horn made her jump. She'd forgotten all about Matias. She held up her hand toward him. "Thank you, Sandra. I appreciate you explaining, but—"

"Mom. Stop. Okay? Just stop." Fabi stepped close. "You know why I wanted to come back here? It wasn't just because I love this city, or because it's where Dad used to live and where Abuela is now. It's because I missed you. The real you. The person you were before we moved to L.A. and you got so busy that I felt like you forgot me half the time. I missed the happy mom who was busy but still made time for my games, made my favorite meals, and who was always there to talk or listen or just hang out." She moved even closer and met Adela's eyes. "This week, I got to be with my mom again—the mom I love and don't want to ever lose. For a while I thought she was gone forever, but I think I found her again. Please don't go to Europe?"

Pain nearly ripped Adela's heart in two. She felt as though a razor-edged arrow had been plunged into her chest and twisted. She'd hurt her baby girl, and she hadn't even realized how much until now. If she went to Europe, would she lose this daughter's respect forever? She wanted that closeness too, more than anything that Europe could offer. Only a fool would walk away from this kind of relationship. A memory of David's face flitted across her memory again. She'd sent him away and ruined any chance at a happy future with him, but she wouldn't make the same mistake with Fabi.

The car door slammed a few yards away, and Matias stormed toward them. "What is going on with you, Adela? Do you realize how late we're going to be? You need to be at the airport at least two hours early, and we'll be lucky if we come close to that. Come on. Let's go."

Adela narrowed her eyes. "Wait a second, Matias—"

"You're out of seconds. Get in the car, Adela. You made your decision. Now let's go."

She looked from Fabi to Sandra to Matias and took a step toward Fabi.

"This is our—your last chance with the network. If you blow this off, you won't just be losing Europe, you'll probably lose *Alta Cocina* too. Is that what you want?"

Her jaw tightened, and she knew with every fiber of her being that it was exactly what she wanted. "I don't care anymore, Matias. My family is more important than my career." She took another step toward Fabi and wrapped her arm around her glowing daughter.

"What? Wait! What did you say? You can't mean that." Matias looked like he was going to stomp his foot but barely contained himself.

"Oh, I do mean it. Absolutely."

Fabi turned to her and threw her arms around Adela's neck, her laughter turning to sobs.

Adela patted her daughter's back and made soothing noises. Then she raised her head and looked straight at her agent. "I'm done, Matias."

"You'll never work in Hollywood again if you do this! You'd better get that clear in your head. And if you're done, where does that leave me? Have you thought about anyone other than yourself?" He reached into the car, pulled out Adela's bag and placed it on the sidewalk nearby.

"Yes, I have. I've thought about myself for way too long, and now I'm thinking about my family. I no longer need a manager. You, Matias, are fired, and are free to go find another star to push around."

Fabi fist pumped as he got into his car, slammed the door, and drove away. "Way to go, Mom! I never did like that man. I'm so glad you're staying. I think we're finally home now."

Adela ruffled Fabi's hair. "Thank you, baby. I couldn't agree more. This is definitely home."

Sandra cleared her throat. "I'm really glad you're staying too, Adela. Romero's needs you, and I think I can learn a lot from you and Soccoro." She shot Fabi a grin. "And maybe even a little from this pip-squeak."

"Hey!" Fabi lightly punched her arm. "Thanks for driving me here to rescue Mom."

"No problem, squirt. But we'd better get back to Romero's before Soccoro has a meltdown. She's going to have her hands full when customers start coming in. Adela, you'll ride back with us, right?"

Adela glanced at the food truck as an idea struck. "Would you give me a minute and then drop me off on the way? I can walk the rest of the way to Romero's, but I have an apology I need to make first."

Fabi grinned and hooted. Adela felt her face warm, but she strode over to the order window as happiness— and a bit of trepidation—flooded her heart.

SANDRA SAT BEHIND the steering wheel of her pickup parked near Victor's food truck with the windows down. What a day! Her mind swirled with all that had happened. Even though much had been bad, ending things with her family on a positive note had been a huge blessing. With the air cleared between them, Adela and Fabi and things at the diner under control, it was time to fill Victor in on how things had turned out with her family.

Victor walked to the back of his food truck and waved. He sauntered up to her window. "I've been thinking about you. You okay?"

"I am. Thank you for your wise counsel earlier."

"Everything is okay with your family now?"

"Yes. They accepted my apology." She blew out a breath. Clarity had come to her. She wanted Victor to be part of her life and not only in moments of crisis or friend dates to prove a point to her grandmother. "Here's the thing. I think you're pretty great, and I'd like to get to know you as more than a friend." She held her breath.

Silence.

Her pulse amped and her face heated. "Umm. Maybe I shouldn't have said that."

"Why not? I feel the same way, but you took me by surprise. I thought you were set on keeping me and all men at arm's length. You said your career was your number one priority."

She nodded. "It was. But I had an epiphany. I like you a lot." Her gaze met his unwavering eyes. "I realized that throwing everything I have into Romero's was keeping me from living a full life. It's like I woke up from a bad dream and finally have clarity."

A wide grin covered his face. He reached for the door handle and pulled open her door.

"What are you doing?"

He took her hand and drew her from the cab of her pickup, guiding them to the sidewalk. "This." He touched her cheek and slowly drew close.

Her eyelids closed in anticipation of Victor's kiss. His warm breath caressed her face. His lips brushed hers. She opened her eyes and ran her hands up his chest, entwining her fingers behind his neck.

His lips caressed hers. He spoke close to her ear. "I want to cook for you."

She leaned her head back. "I'd like that. You're a great cook."

"True."

She laughed. "And humble too."

He stepped back and dipped his chin. "Do you have plans for this evening? Maybe we can catch a movie?"

She sucked in her bottom lip and bit down. "It's been a rollercoaster of a day. Raincheck?"

"Sure." A flicker of disappointment filled his eyes. "Tomorrow?"

"Absolutely."

His smile reached his eyes, and he lowered his head again.

# Chapter Twenty-Five

DAVID PUSHED BACK FROM HIS DESK at his cubicle at work and stretched. The last few hours had dragged and no matter how long he stared at the screen, the words wouldn't come. He kept seeing Adela's face—the sadness in her eyes and the way she'd refused to meet his gaze most of the time at Romero's. Had she really meant what she said about not wanting a relationship with him? That she was done and heading for Europe? He'd been so sure she felt the same way about him that he did about her— he was falling for her, and he couldn't reconcile her actions and words with those feelings, not at all.

A mouth-watering fragrance drifted through the air and made him sit up and sniff. What was that? Lengua tacos? He shook his head. It couldn't be. Although it was possible someone had brought them to work for a late lunch, he supposed. He stood and peered over his cubicle wall. "Who stopped at Tacos Rápidos? Man, not fair to bring those in here and make everyone drool."

"I did!" Adela was striding toward him holding up two takeout bags.

Coworkers peeked around cubicle walls, looking from Adela to David and back. Smiles began to appear before heads pulled back in.

David took a slow step toward her, his heart pounding in his chest. She was the last person he'd expected to see here, today or any other day. "I thought you were leaving town? Did you delay your trip until tomorrow?" He stretched to the side to gaze behind her. "Where's Fabi? She's going to Europe with you, isn't she?"

She slowed, stopped a few feet away, and a small frown creased her brows. "You want a taco? I know you have a lot of questions, but if you have a minute or two, I promise I'll answer them." She bit her lip. "That is, if you want to eat—or even talk to me."

"I'd love one, thank you." He beckoned to the chair across from his at the desk. "Of course, I want to talk to you. I am just surprised to see you here, that's all. You gave me the distinct impression you weren't interested in talking to me again, and that you were leaving town—and the country—later today."

She handed him one of the two bags as she sank into the chair. "I know. I understand why you'd feel that way, and I'm so sorry about how I treated you at Romero's." She dropped her head and then raised it. "I've had so much going on—so many things I needed to sort out in my mind and my head—and I never expected to meet someone like you while I was here." She gave him a soft smile. "I guess I mean, to meet someone again—since we actually first met years ago. Can you forgive me?"

He set his food back to the side and leaned forward, his arms on his desk, his heart rate picking up speed again. Dare he hope she meant what it sounded like? No, he wasn't going to assume anything. That's how he got burned last time. "What do you mean, like me?"

"It was really hard for me to get over my husband and move forward with my life. Before I met you, being with someone—anyone else—seemed impossible. The thing is, David, I like you...a lot. It might even be headed for something more. I thought you might want to know that I'm moving back to San Antonio, so if you ever want to consider asking me out again..." She looked the other direction as color rushed into her cheeks.

He reached across the desk, took one of her hands, then stood and moved around to stand in front of her. "Did I just understand that you've come to care for me— that I might have a chance at something stronger than 'like me' in the future?"

She looked up, met his gaze, and nodded. "I said, I might...I mean...yes. I think that's very possible."

He drew her to her feet, pulled her close, and then wrapped her in his arms and bent his head. His kiss was gentle at first, tentative, as he didn't want to scare her away. Could she really have meant that he had a chance— they had a chance for a future together?"

The pressure of her lips increased, and she leaned into him, slipping her arms around his neck and pulling him close.

A fire ignited inside, and David had all he could do not to sweep her into his arms and kiss her non-stop until they were both too breathless to think. His brain was barely functioning at the moment, anyway. He pulled her down onto his lap and his elbow hit the takeout bag, sending it sliding across the desk, headed for the floor.

Cheers erupted from around them. David and Adela pulled apart, her eyes shining and cheeks pink once again. Several of his co-workers stood nearby, peering over cubicle walls and applauding. David dipped his head for one last kiss, and the cheers and laughter rose as he and Adela separated and stood, holding hands and grinning like a couple of love-sick teens.

SANDRA CLOSED THE front door to her house. "Abuela, I'm home." The scent of fish permeated the house. "You cooked again?"

"Sí. I'm in the kitchen. We're having fish tacos."

"Yum." Too bad she'd already eaten. She left her stuff on the table in the entryway and headed for the kitchen. A full taco bar filled the counter. "What's going on? You don't normally go all out like this." There was no way around not eating now.

"Peter will be joining us."

"Oh. Now I get it. Before he arrives, I want to tell you something."

Abuela looked at her with narrowed eyes. "What about?"

"Remember the man that I went out to dinner with?"

"Victor? The basketball coach?"

"Yes. He also owns and operates a food truck that serves Mexican street food." She needed to spit this out fast before she lost her nerve. "We're dating. I really like him a lot."

"Pfft." Abuela waved a hand as if to toss away her

FINDING LOVE IN SAN ANTONIO

declaration. "This is old news. I could tell when I met him you both have the hots for one another."

Sandra's mouth opened. *The hots?* She chuckled. "You are full of surprises tonight, Abuela. Then how come you still tried to set me up on a date with the butcher?"

Abuela shrugged. "He was a backup."

Sandra shook her head. "How about if I take my taco to my room and give you and Peter some alone time?"

Abuela blinked. "That's not necessary. He's not—"

The doorbell rang.

"I'll get it." Sandra strode to the door and swung it open. "Hi."

Peter stood, holding another pie. "Good evening, Sandra. Your grandmother is expecting me."

She stepped aside. "I heard. That pie smells yummy. Abuela is in the kitchen." She escorted him to where her grandmother still stood, having not moved an inch since the doorbell rang. Could her grandmother be nervous? Hmm. Perhaps there was more here than she'd realized.

"Good evening, Delfina."

Abuela nodded. "You brought dessert?"

He placed the pie on the only available spot on the countertop. "I was taught to never show up empty handed."

"That was very thoughtful of you. Did you make it?"

He chuckled. "No, ma'am. I can whip up a batch of cookies, bake a cake, and even make fudge, but I've never been able to make a pie. I will never understand the saying easy as pie."

Sandra cleared her throat. "I actually grabbed dinner

before I came home. It's been an exhausting day. Would the two of you mind if I retreat to my room?"

"That's fine, dear," Abuela said. "There's plenty if you get hungry later."

Peter grinned. "Would you like to take a piece of pie with you?"

Sandra almost laughed but held it in. The man was smooth for an older guy. He clearly didn't want her to come back for food later and interrupt their evening. "Sure." She pulled a knife from the knife drawer, sliced a generous piece then placed in on one of the plates Abuela had on the counter.

Her grandmother held out a fork and a glass of water. "You'll want these."

"Thanks." She stabbed the fork into the pie and fled to her room. The night she'd suggested Peter stop in to share a piece of pie with Abuela, she'd hoped they'd form a friendship so she'd have a bit of space and Abuela might not be so demanding. This had worked out even better than expected. Maybe the reason her grandmother had been trying so hard to set her up with men was because she was lonely and didn't want Sandra to feel the same.

# Chapter Twenty-Six

AT THE END OF A FAST-PACED day, Sandra was ready to kick her feet up and enjoy the latest hit at the movie theater with Victor, but first she needed to make sure the dining area was cleaned at Romero's. The tables were clean and floor had been mopped, all that remained was wiping down the order counter. She strode into the kitchen to rinse her rag.

Adela and Tía Soccoro stood at the grill talking in whispers.

Sandra frowned. Now what was going on? She'd thought everyone was on the same page, and they were a team. The old Sandra would have stewed over this, but things had improved at Romero's since her blowup and subsequent makeup with her family, so she strolled over to the women. "What's going on?"

Soccoro jumped and pressed her hand to her chest. "You startled me."

Sandra resisted rolling her eyes. "Sorry. I didn't mean to scare you. What are the two of you whispering about?"

"You." Adela smiled. "Soccoro has something to tell you."

"I do?" Soccoro's forehead wrinkled.

Adela released an exasperated sigh. "Don't tell me that scare knocked your plan right out of your head.

Soccoro's eyes widened. "Oh! Right." She turned to face Sandra. "Sandra, I would like for you to take over managing Romero's."

A tingle zipped through Sandra. "For real?" She looked to Adela.

"Don't look at me," Adela said. "I'm the chef."

Sandra's focus slipped back to her aunt. "You said I'm too young and lack experience. What changed?"

"You did for starters. I've seen so much growth in you since returning from California. I know you think I wasn't paying attention to all the effort you put into this place, but I was. Recently, I saw a shift in your approach here. You aren't the know-it-all you once were and are more of a team player now. I like that. I'm confident you and Adela will work well together."

Sandra blew out the breath she'd been holding. "I can hardly believe this." She hugged her aunt. "Thank you."

"So, you accept?" Adela asked.

"Yes! Absolutely yes." Her dream was finally coming true.

Soccoro nodded. "Good. Now there are a few things we still need to work out."

Sandra's stomach sank. She should have known there would be a catch.

"For starters I'll be training you in the things that I've always done. Consider yourself a manager in training."

She could live with that. Though she had pretty

much run the place when her aunt was in California, there had to be things Soccoro did that she still needed to learn. "Strong training is a key to success. Thanks." Soccoro could have turned the business over to her and let her figure out things as she went, but learning details that only Soccoro knew would be extremely helpful.

"You're welcome. I know you won't disappoint me," Soccoro said.

Sandra looked around the kitchen. "If business keeps up the way it has been, we should be able to update things back here in the not-too-distant future."

Adela pumped a fist. "Yes!"

They all laughed and joined arms in a circle.

Tía Soccoro met Sandra's eyes then Adela's. "This is the beginning of a fresh start for all of us. I can't wait to see what's to come."

Sandra couldn't wait to tell Victor and Abuela. Good thing she had a date with Victor tonight. She looked at her watch and winced. "I have to go. Victor and I are going to see a movie." She reached for her bag with a change of clothes inside. She didn't want to reek of food on her first "real" date with Victor. She raced toward the bathroom, and her stomach sank. She still hadn't finished cleaning. She turned and nearly ran into Soccoro.

"You go change." Soccoro nudged her toward the restroom. "I'll finish up here. I know I delayed you."

Relief shot through her. "Thank you." She changed in record time, let her hair down and then waved as she headed out the back door to her pickup. A man stood beside her rig. She pulled up short. "Victor?"

He turned holding a bouquet of flowers.

She hustled toward him. "What are you doing here? I thought we were meeting at the cineplex."

"I wanted to surprise you." He handed her the flowers. "You look radiant. Is that a new dress?"

Her face warmed. She looked down at the red sundress she'd changed into. "No. My closet is filled with dresses. It might take a while for you to see them all."

He chuckled. "Noted."

She looked down at the bouquet in her hand. "Daisies are my favorite flower. How'd you know?"

"Lucky guess. I thought it'd be nice to get dinner before the movie and then catch the later showing. Do you mind?"

She smiled. This man had the best ideas. "Not at all." She spotted his car. "You want to drive, or should I?"

"I will." He pulled open the passenger door and she settled inside while he moved to the driver's side.

He closed the door, and they headed out.

"What'd you have in mind for dinner?"

"A pop-up of sorts."

"Cool." Should she wait to tell him about her news or tell him now? Excitement bubbled to almost overflowing. She might burst if she waited. "I have the most exciting news. I was offered the manager position at Romero's."

Victor glanced her way, wearing a huge smile. "Congratulations! I know how much you've wanted to run Romero's. When do you start?"

She chuckled. "I forgot to ask. I'll be the manager in

training to begin with." She couldn't believe how well everything had come together. She had no doubt, making things right with Adela had helped. "In case I forgot to say so before, thank you for the sound advice that day when I was such a mess."

"You're welcome. I'm glad everything worked out for you."

"I have some news of my own."

"What's that?"

His hands tightened on the steering wheel.

Unease filled her.

"I'm moving my food truck. Adela's cooking is impossible to compete with."

Her stomach flip-flopped. She'd miss having him so close even if they were competitors. "I wish you didn't need to move."

"Me too. I'm going to miss my regulars, but there aren't enough of them to keep me in business."

"I understand, and I'm sorry Romero's is the cause."

"You have nothing to be sorry for. I'm happy for Romero's."

"Where are you moving?"

"It's actually pretty exciting. I posted a schedule on my Instagram. Every day I will have a new location. I've talked with all the property owners, and they are all onboard. The location that gets the most business will host my truck."

"What if there isn't a clear winner?"

"I have a secondary list of locations to try until I find the right spot."

MIRALEE FERRELL and KIMBERLY ROSE JOHNSON

"You've really thought this through."

"No choice. The new life Adela added to Romero's hurt my bottom line."

"I'm sorry you were negatively affected. I hope there's no hard feelings."

"None. We would not be here together if there was." He signaled and turned into a residential development. "I was in a rut. Shaking things up is a good thing."

"Then it's a win for both of us." She frowned. "Though I'm going to miss not being able to see you in the middle of the day. I wonder if another food truck will move in on your old territory."

"Hard to say, but if someone does, I hope they offer a different kind of menu than Romero's, or they won't make it."

Sandra felt sad and happy all at the same time. How was that possible? She looked out the passenger window and saw one house after another. "Is the pop-up at someone's house?"

Victor pulled into a driveway. "In a way. It's a pop-up for two. I made us dinner at my place."

"How sweet." Her heart fluttered. Eating at his place seemed more like a fourth or fifth kind of date, but what did she know? She never got past one date with most guys.

Victor led them through a side gate and across a stone path and into her dream backyard. "You have a swimming pool?!"

"You like swimming?"

"More like taking a dip. Your food truck must have

been doing very well." She slapped a hand over her mouth. "I shouldn't have said that. I'm sorry."

He chuckled. "I'm renting this place, but I hope to buy it one day. The owner said he'd work with me." He motioned toward the covered patio where a buffet table was set up with covered banquet-style serving containers. "Dinner is ready and waiting."

"You've been busy." To say she was impressed by his effort was an understatement. "You sure know how to make a girl feel special."

"Good." He removed the lids with a dramatic flair. "Ta-da. For our meal this evening we have *coq au vin*."

"Fancy! How is it you cook street food when you can make food like this?"

He chuckled. "You better try it first." He prepared two plates and took them to a nearby round table that could seat up to four. "I made iced tea too." He pulled out a chair for her.

She sat. "I can't believe you did all of this."

He shrugged away her comment and reached for her hand. He bowed his head. "Father, we thank You for our many blessings and for this food. Amen."

Sandra opened her eyes. "Amen."

Victor watched her every move.

"You're making me nervous." Her face heated, and she dipped her chin.

"How do you think I feel. I'm dying to know what you think."

"Oh." She loaded her fork with a roasted potato that dripped in wine sauce and tasted it. An explosion of flavor filled her mouth. "It's excellent."

"You didn't try the chicken. Did it get dried out?"

She laughed. "You could try your own." She cut off a small piece and tasted the chicken. "I love it. You're holding out on the world."

"Whew." He dug into his meal.

About halfway through their meal, the lights around his yard came to life, creating a magical oasis. Sandra sighed with contentment. "I don't think I'd ever leave this place if it was mine. It's so peaceful here."

"Yeah. I wish I had more time to enjoy it. Have you heard from Mya lately?"

"Not for a couple of days. Why?"

"Tate is really into her. Just wondered if she mentioned him."

Sandra placed her fork down and sat back. "All I know is she had a great time when we had dessert. We've both been busy and missed our standing coffee date this week."

"That's probably why she hasn't returned his call."

Sandra blinked. "Tate called her, and she didn't respond? I wonder if he called the wrong number?" Mya had told her Tate said he'd call and never did. She thought maybe he'd given her the brushoff. "Hold on." Sandra shot off a quick text to check on her friend and let her know Tate had tried to reach her. Mya responded quickly that all was well, but she was in a class and couldn't talk. "Hmm. Well, it seems she's fine, but indisposed. When did he call?"

"Earlier today."

"Oh. That explains it. Mya's in a class today. She

takes continuing education classes for cosmetology every now and then."

Victor leaned back and reached for his phone. "Tate will be relieved. He thought they'd hit it off, but he hadn't contacted her for over a week because he was in the middle of parent-teacher conferences."

"Speaking of new couples—my grandmother is on a date tonight with our next-door neighbor."

"Good for her."

"Right?" She still couldn't believe Abuela and Peter were a thing. "I've never known my grandmother to date anyone."

"Must be something in the air." Victor reached across the table for her hand and gave it a gentle squeeze.

They finished their meal in comfortable silence.

Sandra placed her fork on her empty plate. She was stuffed about halfway through, but the food was too delicious to leave on the plate. "I know this is going to sound crazy, but I'm so glad my grandma set me up on that horrible date with Anthony. If she hadn't, I never would have been in the parking lot that day we officially became friends."

Victor nodded. "I've thought about that too. Though I didn't realize it was the day that changed everything."

"Let's just say it's when I really noticed you as more than the competition."

Victor checked the time on his phone. "We should get going if we're going to make the movie."

"Would it be okay if we hung out here instead? I can't remember the last time I was so relaxed."

"Sure. I have some board games. Let me clear the table and grab them."

She stood. "I'll help."

"Not tonight. I want you to feel like a princess, and they don't bus tables."

Sandra sat back down. "Mission accomplished." Victor's prayer from earlier about their blessings settled in her mind as she waited for him to return with games. They had both been blessed in so many ways. She looked forward to seeing what the future held for them and had a good feeling she'd finally found her true love.

Victor walked back outside, holding a stack of games.

Her heart skipped a beat. She stood and relieved him of the stack, placing them onto the table.

"What are you doing?" Confusion filled Victor's eyes.

"Shh." She touched his lips with a finger and then pressed her lips softly to his.

His eyes twinkled as he looked down at her. "What was that for?"

"A thank you for tonight. It was perfect."

He kissed the tip of her nose. "I'm glad, but it's about to get better. I have Scrabble…"

Definitely the man of her dreams. Though he might not know it yet, she knew in her heart they had an amazing future together.

# Chapter Twenty-Seven

*Three months later...*

A SMALL FILM CREW STOOD IN the back of the kitchen on the set designed to look like Romero's, cameras pointed at Adela as she took a tray of tamales out of the oven. She smiled into the camera as she placed the tray on the counter. She had never dreamed she'd be able to still have her cooking show and live in San Antonio where her heart and family resided. God had been so good to her and Fabi. Several times, her faith in Him had slipped, but He'd answered her prayers even when she hadn't always known what to say.

She suddenly realized she'd been silent for a heartbeat too long so she smiled again and waved one hand in the air. "Once you take the tamales out of the oven, let them cool for a bit. Then griddle them. Garnish with a little cheese and oregano and *ahí está*! Your pork belly tamales are ready for *your* belly." Quiet laughter rippled around the room. She took a tamale from the tray and took a bite. "Mmm. Perfect. Thank you for watching *Romero's Cocina*. Until next time. Adios!"

"Cut. That's a wrap." Her new director walked up to the counter and patted her shoulder. "Great stuff, Adela.

This new series is way more accessible than *Alta Cocina*. I think I could actually cook the dishes you've been presenting, and I don't cook."

Adela nodded. "That's the point. Now if we're finished for today, *nos vamos*. It's time for me to get to work and cook for real people." She cleaned up quickly and rushed to her car, thankful once again the set was only minutes from Romero's. The Lord had blessed her, indeed.

As soon as she entered the kitchen, she glanced around the room, cherishing the photos on the walls from the past, but ready to move into her future, whatever that might hold. A small smile tugged at her lips as her thoughts returned to David. A framed copy of the recent interview he'd done with her that hit the paper hung in a place of honor. The past three months had almost been a whirlwind courtship, while at other times it seemed like it might not go past the point where they'd landed recently. Comfortable, safe, thrilling, and tantalizing, all at the same time. She wasn't wanting to rush things, but she thought she might be getting close to settling down — she'd made peace with her past and was more than ready to jump feetfirst into her future.

A few minutes later, she was tying her apron when Sandra hurried into the room. "Hey, Adela. Good to see you back."

"Thanks. What's up, boss?"

Sandra rolled her eyes. "Will you stop calling me that? I'm the manager-in-training, remember?"

Adela laughed, loving that she and Sandra were

finally on better terms with all the tension gone this past few months. "Right. But I'm guessing that won't be for much longer. You've been doing a fabulous job with Romero's."

Color rose in Sandra's cheeks, and she dipped her head in acknowledgment. "I appreciate that. I was hoping you'd have time to go over the new additions to the menu soon."

"Let me guess. They're too expensive?" It appeared some things never changed, but she'd have to get used to working on a tighter budget. Sandra really had done a great job during her time as manager, and Adela figured it would get better as time went on and their regular clientele grew.

"Well, yeah, but I may have a lead on an organic farmer who might work with us on his produce prices. Apparently, the guy is in love with our chicharron nachos, so we have that going for us." She grinned. "Every little bit helps, right?"

Soccoro appeared behind Sandra. *"Dónde estás?* We need to get to the bank meeting, and we don't want to be late. I want them to know your face down there whenever you come in. You ready to go?"

Sandra whirled around, her eyes alight. *"Voy!"*

Soccoro raised a brow. "Gracias." She turned to Adela. "What time does Fabi's game start tonight? I don't want to miss it."

"Seven o'clock." Excitement rushed through Adela. Finally, an entire season where she wouldn't have to miss a single one of her daughter's matches. This never would have happened if she'd returned to L.A. or taken the job in Europe. A deep contentment settled over her. Plus, David was coming tonight. It was hard to believe the turn her life had taken and the wonderful man who'd stepped into it. "The season opener. I can hardly wait!"

DAVID SETTLED INTO a seat next to Adela, his heart in his throat as he fingered the small box in his pocket. Was it too soon? Would her family approve? He swallowed hard. More importantly, would Adela approve, or would she shake her head, smile, and tell him she wasn't ready for such an important commitment? There was only one way to find out. Now if he could make it through this game without losing his nerve.

The game went from flying by when Fabi assisted in scoring goals to dragging whenever he'd look at his watch and think about what was ahead. His stomach wouldn't allow him to eat any of the snacks the others had brought to munch on, and Adela kept throwing him worried glances. "You okay?" She nudged him with her elbow. "Aren't you enjoying Fabi's game? You seem a million miles away?"

He mustered the biggest grin possible and slipped his arm around her shoulders. Peace settled over him when she snuggled closer and put her head against his. "I'm fine. I'm glad Fabi's friend from this summer came to watch. He seems like a nice kid."

"Brandon?" She sat up a little straighter but

remained in his embrace. "Yeah, Fabi has invited him to the house a couple of times, and he's great. She's only a freshman in high school this year, though, so I'm not crazy about her rushing into a relationship."

"She has a wise mother and grandmother to guide her, and she has a solid head on her shoulders. I think she'll make good decisions."

She sighed. "I hope so. I didn't always make the best ones at her age, but things seem to have turned out well for me now, right?" She gave him a cheeky smile and kissed his cheek.

"Right." He pulled her closer with one arm and put his other hand back in his jacket pocket to make sure the box hadn't disappeared. Nope. Still there. He drew in a deep breath. They were in the last quarter. Not much time to go. "Hey, will you take a walk with me after the match ends? I have something I want to show you." He'd almost said ask you, but he didn't want her to start asking questions.

She eyed him speculatively and nodded. "Sure. I'd like that. Since I rode over with you, Soccoro and Fabi won't worry about me if I'm late." Her eyes twinkled in the artificial light beaming over the stadium. "In fact, I'm guessing they'd be upset with me if I rushed straight home."

He hoped that meant her family was rooting for a continued romance between the two of them, but he wasn't going to jinx things by asking. No, better to wait until the proper moment and see how it all played out.

IN THE LAST minute of the game, Fabi kicked the ball straight into the goalie net and scored. The crowd rose to their feet and cheered. Adela jumped up and down, clapping and screaming until she thought she'd lose her voice. Her baby had done it! She'd scored the winning goal in a very tight game and put herself in an excellent position for the rest of the season. Her dad would have been so proud of her. She was suddenly aware that the thought of Mauricio didn't come with any pain or sense of loss, just pride. When had that happened? She turned to David and threw her arms around his neck and kissed him.

He returned the kiss with slow deliberation and then pulled back a few inches as people started exiting the stands. "What was that for? Not that I minded at all, but something felt...different...I don't know how to explain it."

She smiled. "Something in here..." she patted her chest over her heart... "changed a minute ago. I was thinking how proud Fabi's dad would have been of her, and I only felt joy—no sadness—no regret or pain. I think I'm finally healed and ready to move on."

HE WHISTLED LONG and low. This couldn't be better timing. He saw Fabi racing toward the stands and stifled a grin. Maybe a walk wasn't the best place for this. After all, he wanted Fabi's approval as well. He took Adela's hand, pulled her down the side aisle to the grass, and then stopped, put his hand back in his jacket pocket, and sank to one knee, still holding Adela's hand.

Out of the corner of his eye, he saw Fabi almost stumble to a stop as she drew close, her eyes wide and inquiring, but a small smile tugged at her lips. He met her gaze briefly, and she gave him a nod then stopped and waited, as though she knew exactly what he planned.

"Adela." He brought the back of her hand to his lips, pressed them against it, then turned it over and lay her palm against his cheek, cherishing the warmth and comfort it brought. "I know it hasn't been a long time since we started dating, but I think I fell in love with you way back when we were seventeen and working in Romero's. That's why there's never been anyone else in my life that's been serious. Your memory kept that from happening." He gazed up at her.

Her mouth formed a little O but she didn't pull her hand away, just nodded and smiled, as though encouraging him to continue.

"Whether I was in love with you back then or not, I know I am now. The thought of having you in my life forever is amazing—so much so I can barely contain the joy I feel over it, or the fear I feel thinking what I'd do if I lost you." He turned his head a few inches to include Fabi in the next question. "I'm wondering if Fabi and you would allow me to be part of your family?" He placed all of his attention back on Adela. "What I'm trying to say and not doing a very good job of it, is would you marry me?"

Several heartbeats passed with Adela just looking at him with a soft glow shining from her eyes. Suddenly, Fabi let out a little squeal. 'Yes, yes, yes! She'll marry you!" She jumped up and down, clapping and screaming, until people walking away turned to see what had happened. A few smiles lit faces as they stared from Fabi to him kneeling in front of Adela and back to Fabi.

Fabi's response seemed to jar Adela out of her trance. "Hey, he's asking me to marry him, not you, young lady." She grinned at Fabi. "But I'm very glad I have your approval." She turned her attention back to David and slowly sank to her knees in front of him. "Thank you for being so patient with me. Thank you for giving me the time I needed to heal and for not demanding more than I was ready to give. And thank you for asking me here—in this very special spot that means so much to my daughter—and for including her in the decision. I couldn't be prouder or happier to say yes. I'd love to become your wife. And the sooner the better!"

Joy exploded inside him, and he stood to his feet, drawing her up. He caught her in his arms and swung her around. They stopped next to Fabi who threw her arms around them both, alternating between almost hysterical laughter and tears. "It's about time, you two. I thought you'd never get your act together. I get to be your maid of honor. I'm too old to be a flower girl."

Laughter erupted from David and Adela at the same time, and they both pulled Fabi into a big hug. They'd found love and expanded their family—all in San Antonio—the city of her heart and her hope for the future.

# Connect with Miralee and Kimberly

Visit Kimberly's website at kimberlyrjohnson.com

Find more books by Kimberly on Amazon at
www.amazon.com/default/e/B00K10CR6E

Visit Miralee's website and sign-up for her newsletter at
www.miraleeferrell.com

Find more books by Miralee on Amazon at
https://www.amazon.com/Miralee-Ferrell/e/B001JS7ZTQ

CPSIA information can be obtained
at www.ICGtesting.com
Printed in the USA
LVHW030044040522
717733LV00014B/488